TREE BY LEAF
CYNTHIA VOIGT

Winner of the Newbery Medal for *Dicey's Song* and a Newbery Honor for *A Solitary Blue*

"Complex, beautifully structured . . . Rewarding for thoughtful readers."

The Kirkus Reviews

"Voigt's novel is a rich character study with a strong period flavor. She presents a convincing and dramatic portrayal of the class and cultural distinctions that operated at the time."

Booklist

"Voigt has woven together her themes of love, war and loss. . . . Miraculously convincing and moving."

Publishers Weekly

Also by Cynthia Voigt
Published by Fawcett Juniper Books:

TREE BY LEAF

Cynthia Voigt

FAWCETT JUNIPER • NEW YORK

RLI: $\dfrac{\text{VL 5 \& up}}{\text{IL 6 \& up}}$

A Fawcett Juniper Book
Published by Ballantine Books
Copyright © 1988 by Cynthia Voigt

Library of Congress Catalog Card Number: 87-17512

ISBN 0-449-70334-7

This edition published by arrangement with Atheneum Publishers, an imprint of Macmillan, Inc.

Manufactured in the United States of America

First Ballantine Books Edition: March 1989

Peter—remember walking across the bridge by Robin's house one summer night? Remember what you asked me? I think this is my way of asking that same question; I know it's my way of remembering walking across the bridge with you, hearing you ask it.

1

SILENCE. Except for her footsteps, except for the soft thunk of mussels dropped onto the rocks by gulls, except for the wind that moved murmuring through the distant trees above her, there was silence. The tide had slipped out, leaving mud flats bare and mussel beds exposed. Her skirts tangled at her legs. As Clothilde walked on, following the curving beach, her skirts made a weak echo of the sound of the breeze.

At the far end of the beach, boulders lay piled upon each other, great masses of rock abandoned eons ago by retreating glaciers. Clothilde climbed up behind a chunk of granite. The quiet enfolded her. She put down the slatted clam basket and the thick-tined rake. Leaning against the rock, she pulled off her rubber boots, first the right and then the left. She took off the heavy socks Mother made her put on under the boots. They were Father's socks, too big for her. In the corner of the attic were four trunks of Father's clothes, packed away—shirts, trousers, coats, sweaters, waistcoats, ties, long johns and nightshirts, socks, boots and shoes. Clothilde balled up the second sock in her hand and dropped it onto a flat ledge of rock. She hoisted her skirt to unfasten the petticoat underneath, pulled the petti-

coat down and off, shook it out and folded it neatly on top
of the socks. Reaching through her legs, she took the back
hem of her skirt and pulled it forward, tucking it into its
waistband at the front. She rolled up the long loose sleeves
of her blouse.

Some day, Clothilde thought, clambering up, working
her way along the familiar invisible path, she would like to
strip down to her shift and drawers. She could do it.
Nobody would know. Once she was out of sight of the
house she could be entirely alone. Mother could call and she
wouldn't hear. Mother could ring the old hand bell until her
arm fell off, but Clothilde wouldn't hear it.

Above the boulders, the woods crowded up to the land's
end. Once within the trees, Clothilde moved quickly. *Mine,*
her bare feet said, landing surely—*Mine,* her heart beat
strongly; running around her body her blood said it too—
Mine, Mine. It was, too, it was hers, the whole mitten-
shaped peninsula.

She stayed within the woods. She had marked the way
with little cairns of piled stones, but she didn't need
markers. Her feet had worn it down until it was as distinct
as a deer's path, and her eyes found it easily. If she had
gone farther inland, she could have made better time on the
dirt road that ran beside the fields, but Clothilde preferred
her own path. Pines, the older ones towering up high, grew
thick and straight. Slender white birches clustered together
among the pines. A few maples and spruces were scattered
through the pines and birches. Underneath, on the soft pine
needles, ferns flourished in the shade, and mosses spread
out. Sometimes, one of her own cairns, no more than three
fist-sized rocks arranged in a way that would look natural to
the careless eye, marked the path; sometimes she had used
one of the boulders that thrust up through the ground.

She didn't run through the woods. She walked—avoiding
branches and prickly scrub growth, her ears hearing the
waving of branches in the wind, her eyes seeing the dappled

sunlight moving through the trees. She moved through patches of sunlight and patches of shade. Sunlight and shade ran over her, like the water in one of the little falls that cascaded down the rocky headlands after a rain.

When she reached the easternmost point of land, Clothilde sat down on a ledge of rock, with the trees close behind her. Here, the boulders made a steep slope she could climb down, if she wanted, to sit on whatever rock was at the water's edge. Here the tides moved up and down over the rocks, always moving, rising tides or falling tides. Some of the boulders had clumps of seaweed growing on them, long yellowy-brown air-pocketed strands crowded out from the center.

Around here, they called it rockweed, not seaweed. At first, Clothilde had refused to call it that, and then she had changed and called it rockweed, and now she had stubbornly gone back to her old name for it, the name she had first learned. *Seaweed,* she'd say, knowing she was going to be corrected. *Seaweed,* she'd say, wanting whoever she was talking to to know that she wasn't going to change what she named it even if everybody here tried to make her. They couldn't know that—like a word you learned you'd been spelling wrong so that ever after when you started to spell it you contradicted and confused yourself and never were sure if you were right—inside her head she called it *rockweed, no, seaweed*. Not that she talked to anybody much. Not that anybody cared what she called it.

Away to the east, beyond the two little islands that lay so close to shore that she could make out trees and coves, and the clear, white, round lighthouse, beyond the three dark shapes, which were outlying islands, lay the Atlantic Ocean, and beyond that Europe—England, France, Belgium. The water, so clear beneath her that she could see the colors of underwater rocks and the floating fingers of seaweed out afar, rippled under the breeze into a blue field that struck gold from the sun, rippling gold as it moved. The sky was clear above, with only a few little fluffy white clouds drifting aimlessly across it. The sun poured warm over Clothilde where she sat with her bare legs against the rough stone, with the woods rustling behind her. *Mine,* she thought, her imagination picturing the entire peninsula, *Mine.*

And it was. She didn't know why Great-Aunt Clothilde, Grandfather's ill-liked sister, had left it to her, unless it was her name. She didn't even care why the three-hundred-and-fifty-acre, mitten-shaped peninsula was hers, and only hers. Clothilde had met her great-aunt just once, and she had no memory of the meeting. She had been only three or four at the time, the time years ago when Grandfather had reluctantly asked his sister to dinner, since she had come to Boston to revise her will. That must have been the time when she decided to give the peninsula to Clothilde, but there was no answer to the question Why. The will had simply said, after everything else, "To my great-niece Clothilde I leave that property known as Speer Point, Maine, and all the buildings upon it." The big summer cottage Great-Aunt had built had burned down, long before Clothilde had gotten there, maybe even before her great-aunt had died. The only remaining buildings were the farm manager's house they lived in, at the curve where the mitten's thumb began, and a dilapidated boathouse across the peninsula, close to where the big summer cottage had stood. Where the cottage had stood, at the knuckle below the mitten's little finger, tall blackened timbers pointed up into the sky like scorched bones, a mass of burned rubble rotted away, and one glass wall, all that was left of the conservatory, collapsed more every year. Nobody knew how the cottage had burned—maybe tramps, maybe children, maybe lightning. Clothilde had gone to look at the ruin, just once. It was too much like war and she never went again.

The whole peninsula was hers, and it lay behind her like

a right-hand mitten, a mitten with a terribly narrow wrist where the high causeway road led away to the village. Clothilde would have preferred an island, but a peninsula—almost an island in the Latin Mother made her study with Nate—was good enough. Especially if it was all hers: the acres of overgrown fields, where Queen Anne's lace and black-eyed Susans grew among the long grasses, and the two tilled fields, land they traded to Mr. Henderson for milk and butter; the high rocky blueberry fields at the center of the peninsula; and the woods, acres of timber. The peninsula was her future. Lumber companies always wanted to buy timber. The woods, felled and transformed, cut into poles for telegraph and telephone wires, sliced into boards, chipped into shingles, cooked into a pulp for paper, or carved into furniture—the peninsula gave her a future.

Clothilde couldn't sit for long that day, much as she would have liked to. The tide was still going out, but soon it would turn and begin to edge up along the rocks below and slide back into the cove. She had clams to dig and she couldn't linger long. She sat for a few minutes longer, even so. She didn't think about anything. She watched and listened and let the sun shine on her bare head and bare arms, with no more will than one of the flat jellyfish the tide sometimes left stranded on the beach. It wasn't really like a mitten, her peninsula, Speer Point. It wasn't smooth edged at all. If there was a hand it had actually been knitted to fit, that was a monster's hand with lots of sharp pointy fingers crowding out of the knuckles and a huge disproportionate thumb, and the scrawny wrist about one narrow bird-bone thick. If there really was such a hand, and you saw it, it would be so bad you'd have to turn your face away and pretend it wasn't there, or look at it and feel so sorry you'd want to just weep. Or get angry—at the mother and father for having the monster, or at the whole world that included it, or at God. The peninsula was really a thick monster hand of land, clawing out into the sea with sharp little fingers.

She supposed it was ugly—remote, uncultivated, grown wild—but that didn't matter because it was hers. Besides, she knew it was beautiful.

God had done such good work on land and trees, oceans, mountains, islands, and the firmament with its two great lights, the way the Bible said it, one for the day and one for the night. He'd done so well with everything else, He could have done better with people. And He should have. If she were God, she wouldn't have made people at all. If she were God, she'd have stopped with everything that creepeth, and she'd have kept the Garden of Eden for herself, and there never would have been such a thing as war. If she were God, Clothilde thought, she'd have known better.

As silent as one of the Indians that used to inhabit the coast, Clothilde got up and made her way back through the trees. Silent as the still water, quiet as one of the Indians from the lost tribes, Clothilde moved through the trees. She climbed back down the boulders.

By comparison, the beach was noisy. Gulls squabbled and the mud made thick sucking sounds at the boots she had put back on, over the thick socks. When she found a group of little air holes, Clothilde set down the clam basket. She leaned her weight on the rake, forcing the tines down into the flat mud. The mud didn't want to be dug up and tried to hold itself together, separating from itself with the same sucking sounds with which it released her boots. The rake was as much a shovel as a rake. It was really a short thick shovel, with heavy metal tines instead of a flat bottom. It was made that way so it could dig efficiently but not cut through any more clams than it had to, as it lifted the mud and dumped it down.

Clothilde stood with her feet set wide apart and dug a shallow pit between them. That turned up a few clams, which she tossed into the basket beside her. Those clams with shells crushed into by the tines of the rake she tossed aside. Maimed and broken, the pale pulpy flesh bared to the air, they were already dead, or dying. You couldn't tell which, with clams. Clothilde didn't mind digging clams, didn't mind cooking them alive, because they were food. But she minded those clams the rake smashed. There should be a better way to dig clams.

When the trench between her feet was finished, she leaned forward to force the rake deep into the mud, then pulled. The miniature cliff collapsed toward her; she bent over and worked her fingers through the mud, to find the hidden clams. They didn't need all that many clams to make Sunday chowder for the five of them. Cooked on Saturday evening, the chowder ripened up overnight. They would eat it for dinner tomorrow, a soup as thick as a stew with its chunks of potatoes and its clams, a rich milky fishy stew. Clothilde leaned over and pulled, bent down to find out the clams that had backed themselves down into the mud, moved to a new area pitted with air holes and began again.

She was perspiring. Her blouse stuck to her back. Her hands and arms, like the rake and basket, were streaked with gray clayey mud. Clothilde didn't mind that. She liked the sharp, salty smell and the thick streaks of mud. She liked the tiredness. When she had gathered enough clams, she picked up the basket and walked on out to where the water had gotten to, in its rising, set the basket down, bent over to splash water on her hands and arms, and her face too. The water was cool, cold. It wasn't icy, because the July sun warmed the mud flats enough to heat the water as it returned into the cove, but it was definitely cold. Her steps loosened mud from the bottom and it rose like underwater dust, until the moving water cleared it away. Looking at the bottom, Clothilde saw how the waves made wavy diamond shapes out of the sunlight. Those diamonds chased themselves restlessly over the floor of the cove. There were too many, they moved too quickly, like the little waves on the water's surface.

The water had rinsed the thickest mud off the clams, and

Clothilde used her palms and fingers to finish the job.
Mother would give the clams a final cleaning in the kitchen
sink. The sun was moving along the sky, the tide was
slipping into the cove, and Clothilde knew she was already
later than she should have been. Picking up the heavy
basket, splashing back to the rake to carry it in her other
hand, she returned to the beach. She pulled her petticoat
back on and shook her skirt out over it, so it would hang
properly. She rolled down the sleeves of her blouse. She
didn't want to go back.

She didn't want to go back because when she was alone
on the beach, in the woods, at the headlands especially, but
anywhere in her wanderings over the peninsula, Clothilde
was as close to happy as she could ever remember being.
Even digging clams or gathering mussels, she felt herself
sitting content in herself. Not worrying the way she often
worried; not reassuring herself the way she often did, by
remembering the peninsula, which was hers. That struck
her as odd, because whenever she thought about digging
clams and gathering mussels she felt a resentment that
burned inside her. Why should she be the one to go out and
gather, to get her hands cut on barnacles and sharp shells,
her palms callused on the handle of the rake, her fingernails
blackened by mud. Nate sometimes brought home fish,
because a gentleman could know how to fish. Sailing a boat
was something a gentleman could know how to do, so he
could sail out and anchor, and bring home fish for dinners.
Dierdre was not quite four, too young to be useful, so it was
Clothilde who chopped wood, year-round, for the stoves,
and shoveled coal into the boiler that supplied hot water for
the house; who dug potatoes out of the garden with Mother;
it was Clothilde who—whose future didn't matter. The
resentment burned like a slow fire in her. And even while it
burned, at the same time and in the same place, contentment
washed over her. The sunny silence wrapped around her
like arms.

Clothilde walked along slowly, partly because of the weight of the clam basket, partly because she was going back. The clam basket pulled at her shoulder and banged against her leg. She reassured herself: she had her plans, she had her peninsula and her plans.

She could have entered the kitchen from the one door at the back of the house, in the ell that connected the farmhouse to its barn, but Clothilde always went around to the front, where the house faced down the driveway. The driveway was only two shallow dirt tracks, with grass growing up between them. It led away through the long grass and into the trees. Because almost nobody came up it, the driveway was overgrown. But when she looked at it, standing by the house, Clothilde could see as clear as if it hadn't happened four years ago, in May of 1916, but yesterday, in July of 1920, how Father had looked riding away west into a setting sun.

He was in uniform by then, riding off to join his cavalry regiment. He sat Bucephalus easily, carelessly. Father was a born horseman, everybody said. Clothilde had seen him a hundred times the way she had seen him that morning, except that he hadn't been in uniform before. Father's back was straight and his smile fell over all of them like sunlight, while the big horse moved restlessly, eager to be going. Father, too, was eager. He turned the horse's head and went off at a fine canter, to please them, to show off. Just before he entered the trees, he unsheathed his sword and swung it over his head. He was teasing, Clothilde and Nate knew, making fun of his soldier self, but he was also proud and gallant, as if right then he could hear bugles blowing to call him into battle, where he and Bucephalus would charge through the enemy, smiting right and smiting left.

Life went easily for Father. Even when he made it hard, it was easy for him, because everyone liked him. He was big and handsome and happy, he had a ready laugh and a strong arm, he was always talking, telling stories on himself. When Father, who had only been there for a day and a night, left the farmhouse to ride off to war, he left the rooms cold and empty behind him, as if the house had already gotten used to him being there and wanted him to stay. But Father had gone.

But sometimes, as if time cracked and let a glimmer of light through from the past, Clothilde could look quickly at the driveway and quickly away, and see Father riding off—and her heart would lift. Recently, she could always see that picture, although the figure on the big horse became less distinct every time. Setting down the heavy basket, holding herself still to catch that glimpse, Clothilde almost really saw it.

2

NOBODY but Lou was in the kitchen. And Lou had the windows wide open to cool down the room. She was heating flatirons on the stove and she had set the ironing board beside the open door. She didn't look up when Clothilde came in.

Clothilde emptied the clams into the sink. She might as well go ahead and give the clams their final cleaning. She guessed she would steam them, too, if Mother didn't show up. She turned on the tap water and scrubbed the pale gray clams, one at a time, one after another, using a vegetable brush. The brush made a small sweeping sound on the clam's shell, water trickled into the sink, the iron swooshed back and forth on the damp clothes, and the trees rustled outside.

Dierdre would still be napping, and Nate had sailed over to have lunch and play tennis at the club in town with one of his friends from Phillips Academy. She hadn't seen Mother in the garden, she was pretty sure Mother wasn't upstairs, and she guessed she knew where Mother had gone. Mother wouldn't stay long there, and when she got back she wouldn't have anything to say. Clothilde washed the clams, then scrubbed at her hands to get the gray mud out from

11

under her fingernails. That done, she ran a little water into
the big steamer and set it on the stove. Lou had the stove
stoked up high for the irons, so Clothilde didn't need to feed
in any more wood. While she waited for the water to come
up to a boil, she sat at the kitchen table.

Lou paid no attention to her. Lou ironed. Her thin, pale
hair was pulled back into a knot at the back of her head. Her
thin arms moved the heavy iron along the skirt of Mother's
blue church dress. The skirt hung down onto the floor,
but that did no harm because Lou scrubbed the painted
floorboards every evening. Lou wasn't much taller than
Clothilde and she wasn't that much older, just fifteen, but
she looked and worked like a woman grown. When Lou
returned the flatiron to the stove and had tested one of the
others with a dampened fingertip, she told Clothilde, "Pot's
steaming," in her flat voice.

Clothilde carried the clams over by handfuls, dumping
them into the pot. She put the lid back on top and sat down
again. It took fifteen minutes to steam clams. She looked at
the clock on the wall.

Lou finished Mother's dress and held it out to see that
there were no wrinkles she'd left. She put the dress on a
hanger and hung it up on the nail by the door. Then she
turned around to look straight at Clothilde. She looked and
looked before she asked her question. "Who is that man in
the boathouse?"

Clothilde looked at the clock. Lou was a servant.
Clothilde didn't have to answer. She didn't want to answer,
didn't want to say, didn't want to think about it. Lou stood
waiting, her jaw out, her pale face without expression, lips,
eyes, and eyelashes pale, and she didn't have any right to
ask. In Grandfather's house, a servant would never have
asked a question like that, and in that way.

"What man?" Clothilde asked.

"Yuh," Lou said. "He's been seen, daytime, and Tom
Hatch was late coming in the other night and he said there

was a light in the boathouse. He was worried about your ma, so he ast me. It's that man I'm asting you about."

Clothilde didn't want to say it. Even having Lou mention him made the day dark, as if a cold gray fog had seeped up into the kitchen from the cellar below. Because she didn't want to say it, the words hurting in her mouth, Clothilde made herself speak. "He's my father."

It was true. There was no use denying that. It frightened her, but there was no use denying it.

Lou thought for a while about what Clothilde had said. Clothilde looked at the clock. She looked at the freshly ironed dress. She looked at her fingers resting on the wood of the table.

"Why's she hiding him away over there?" Lou asked.

"She's not," Clothilde said. Which was true and not true. "She doesn't say."

"Yuh." Lou moved slowly back to the ironing board. Clothilde got up from the table, to set the metal colander over the soup pot, to line the colander with clean muslin. She knew Lou didn't carry tales. The servants in Grandfather's house gossiped, but when Lou went home Sundays to her family, she didn't talk about the people out on the Point. They'd learned that, because whatever trouble they had on them, Mr. Grindle at the store never knew of it. Mr. Grindle didn't know, not until Mother told him, that Nate was going to attend Phillips Academy, where the summer boys from town went to school; and he never suspected that it was Grandfather who sent Nate there, with Mother asking Nate to accept the gift. What Mr. Grindle knew, his eyes showed, if he was sorry for your trouble and glad for your good news, or if there was something he knew you wanted kept secret. Those bulging eyes didn't know anything, nothing they hadn't told him themselves, because Lou wasn't the kind to carry tales from the Point into the village.

Clothilde took a holder to lift the top off the steaming pot. The clams had opened. The steamy air that rose into her face smelled sweet and fishy. She picked up another holder to lift the pot in both hands, carried it over to the sink, and carefully poured its contents out into the colander. Then she sat down again at the table. The broth needed time to drain through the muslin. She watched Lou's thin shoulders move as her arms moved the heavy iron up and down over one of Nate's shirts.

"What did you say to Tom Hatch?" Clothilde asked.

"I told him to mind his own business, yuh," Lou answered, without turning around.

Clothilde could just hear Lou saying that. Poor Tom Hatch would have thought he was just giving them a warning, if a tramp had moved out onto the property and Mrs. Speer there with only her boy for protection, and him only just fourteen. Tom Hatch would have meant well. But Lou must have given him one of her pale-eyed glances all the same, and she'd told him to keep his nose stuck in his own business.

When the clams had stopped steaming up into the air, Clothilde shook the colander a couple of times, in case any broth was trapped in any shells, then lifted it over onto the metal draining rack. She moved the soup pot with its watery broth back to the stove, setting it up high on the warming shelf. She turned around and watched Lou.

Lou held the iron awkwardly, and her hands moving the shirt around on the ironing board looked clumsy, because of her fingers. Lou's fingers had been caught in the looms, more than once, when she worked in the mill in Fall River, and they'd healed up crooked. Lou had clever hands, for sewing and cooking, strong hands for cleaning, even though they looked like she shouldn't be able to do anything. Lou was full of contradictions like that. She was a girl but she seemed a woman grown. She looked pale and weak, but she was strong. She couldn't read or write, but whatever she said made sense, and she was quick to learn. She had a meek and quiet way of behaving, standing as if she hoped nobody would notice she was in a room, as if she'd never dare speak out, but she asked stubborn questions or stubbornly refused to answer. She never complained, even though Clothilde guessed she had plenty to complain about.

Never having had what she'd call a friend, Clothilde wasn't sure of it, but she suspected that Lou would make a good friend, if she hadn't been a servant. As far as Clothilde had observed, you made friends from among the girls you went to school with, because of things that were the same for all of you. Clothilde had always been different from the girls in her school in Manfield, and here too. If those girls in Manfield with their starched pinafores could see her now, she thought, getting up to shuck the clams, she could imagine what they'd say. She didn't care anyway. They didn't know anything, they never did and they always acted like they were so perfect. If Lou had ever been in a school, she wouldn't have acted like that. Those girls wouldn't even know how to shuck clams.

Clothilde pulled at the shell of the first clam until it broke apart. She removed the honey-colored body and peeled off the thin black skin that lay along its side and fitted over its long dark neck. She put the clam into a bowl; the skin she dropped onto the counter. Without having to think about it, she picked up the next. And the girls here, she thought, her fingers working, they wouldn't believe she knew all about how to shuck clams, and dig potatoes, and scrape a mussel clean with a knife, and—a whole lot of things. If she were God, she'd make people differently, she'd make them all plan to like each other, she'd make them all the same.

Empty shells clattered into the sink. Clothilde's hands smelled like cooked clams, a warm, nutty smell.

"Is she afraid of him, then?" Lou's voice asked behind her.

"What?" Clothilde asked. "Who?"

"Him. That man. Your father."

"Afraid?" Clothilde couldn't understand what Lou was thinking of.

"I shouldn't be asting, I shouldn't be thinking about it," Lou's voice said. They were talking with their backs to each other, both of them working at their tasks. "And I wouldn't, except I'm worried about her."

"You mean Mother?"

"It's like she's sickly. You must've noticed it. Maybe I should put my nose right back on my face, but if I found out I could've he'ped her, and I hadn't ast—because she's been so good to me."

Clothilde turned around, confused. The kitchen was a big room, taking up half of the downstairs. The other half was partly the front parlor, and partly the hall where the stairs came down. The kitchen was their main room, with the heat from the range to warm it and the broad table—big enough for a dozen people at one sitting. When the farm had been worked, in Great-Aunt Clothilde's day, there might be a dozen men sitting down for a meal, when the harvest hay was being gathered, or the blueberries were ripe. Her family used the table for study, for extra counter space when they were putting up beans and peas and tomatoes, for laying out patterns to cut fabric—they used it for everything, and eating too. The parlor they only used in the evenings, when Mother read the Gospels to them. If they'd had callers, the parlor would have been used to receive them in. But the kitchen was where they lived.

Finally, Clothilde thought of something she could say. "She didn't help you so much." She didn't think Lou ought to be talking like this and she knew she oughtn't to be listening. *But why not?* she asked herself, angry, *Who says?*

"My ma needs my wages, so she's he'ped," Lou told her, which was surely true. Clothilde had been to where Lou's family lived, and she had seen the need for even the small wage Mother could pay Lou. "And your mother kep' me on, yuh, even after she told Pa he couldn't work for her no longer. He'd been thinking, he'd got a fine place where he'd go Fridays with his hand out and never do nothing because it was only a woman to run it. She sure ripped his ears off, and now—she lets things slip."

Clothilde put the clam she was holding into the bowl, and gave Lou her full attention. Lou was just waiting, holding the iron. "Mother's an orphan," she explained. "She always acted like one until my father went away."

"To the war," Lou said.

Clothilde didn't need any reminding of where Father went. She tried to explain how things were, in Grandfather's house, in Massachusetts. "Before, at my grandfather's house, we lived there but nobody wanted us, except we were Father's." Lou didn't understand. "It was because Mother was a nobody. And a Catholic too. And because they eloped to get married. It was—she was—a shame on the family—we are. She isn't sickly."

"Then why keep him over to the boathouse?" Lou demanded, unsatisfied. Lou couldn't have understood, Clothilde realized. She couldn't know how it had been at Grandfather's house. Lou couldn't know how people could act when they were angry at you, and how they would stay angry for years and years, even when they had money to buy everything they could want and always went to church.

"It's what *he* wants," she said. "He said."

Clothilde thought Lou would go back to her ironing then, but she didn't. There was something more on her mind, something she wanted to ask, or say. Clothilde was afraid of what Lou would ask, but she made herself stand waiting for the question. She knew how to make herself stand quiet, to see what people were going to do, and stay quiet, whatever happened.

"Is he in a bad way, then?" Lou asked. Lou meant, in a bad way like Jeb Twohey, who'd come back home after only three months in France, not wounded but crazy as a bedbug—he'd talk crazy, to people who weren't there about things that weren't happening, until his family kept him to the house. Jeb's in a bad way, people said, feeling sorry for his family. Whenever he came out they'd act like he wasn't there, because if you said anything to him, Jeb's mouth would wrinkle up and he'd burst into tears, or start yelling, or do something crazy like crawl under a table with his hands over his ears and nobody could get him to come out.

Clothilde shook her head, No.

"Yes," Clothilde said.

Then she nodded her head, Yes, and said, "I don't know." She shrugged her shoulders and said, "No." She didn't want to have to think about it.

"Will she be wanting me to move out?" Lou asked. She had her own room in the ell, with a cot and a bureau in it. She'd asked Mother, soon after she'd come to work for them, if she couldn't please sleep in; she'd said she was clean and quiet and would keep out of the way. Mother had given her permission.

"No, of course not." Clothilde had never thought of that possibility. Mother wouldn't do that, would she? Besides, now that Father was back, only he could ask Lou to leave, so Mother couldn't. "Why should she?"

"Because I wouldn't like to leave her, not like this, and I don't want to go back to home, besides. Yuh, that's a sure thing." Lou turned back to her ironing.

Clothilde went back to shucking the clams, her fingers working, her mind working. She wouldn't want to go back to Grandfather's house, never mind how big and fancy it was. If she thought she might have to . . . she'd run away, and hide, and live in the woods. She couldn't have stood to go back there. She didn't want to go back to the school there, where the girls ignored her, or said things in corners for her to hear but never the teacher. What did it mean, anyway, what people said about Catholics? She wasn't one anyway—Mother never went to a Catholic church; she went to the Presbyterian church with Grandfather and Father and the aunts. On the other hand, Clothilde had to admit the school here wasn't any better, so it wasn't just those girls. School here had never been any better and it was worse, since Nate had left. They'd minded his going off to Phillips Academy last fall, although nobody said so to him. Nobody would say so to him, and if they did he'd turn it into a joke. They just said so to her, and the boys who used to be his friends would troop along after her, like a pack of yapping dogs, when she started along home. She hadn't known how it would be, at school, with Nate gone. They said teasing things to her, waiting for her to start to run away. She'd pretend that she couldn't hear a word, pretend she was alone, while they said things about kissing a girl whose brother was going to inherit a factory and be a rich man. They'd come up closer and closer around her. Once, one of them had stopped her and pushed his face into hers—she'd slammed her books into his face, and he was surprised, and *she'd* just laughed. Since then, they'd kept their distance, but they'd gotten meaner. The girls weren't any better. They thought she was stuck up, and teacher's pet, and they moved away if she came to sit near them, which she didn't, any more than she could help. Nate had it easier, because he could fight, he was a boy. Then, when he'd fought out whatever it was, he'd laugh and say let's go do something, let's get some frogs, or race to the church and back. They didn't think Nate was stuck up, and they didn't mind that he was a teacher's pet.

Clothilde didn't think she *was* stuck up, anyway. She didn't mind how small the village school was, just fourteen boys and girls in all the grades together. If there had been more of them there would just have been more people not to like what she wore and said, how she talked and the way her school papers looked. If she had a round face and blue eyes, and bright fluffy dresses, like Polly Dethier, Clothilde thought they'd act different. When boys came up to ask Polly Dethier if they could carry her books, it wasn't so they could drop them into any mud puddle, or run away and hide them in the woods. Clothilde had light brown hair her mother braided every morning into French braids, and a square face; her dresses were made-over skirts worn with white blouses; and whenever she saw Polly, envy ate at her heart. She despised Polly Dethier, who did nothing but act happy and smile, to show off her dimple. She wished she looked like Polly so she could like herself better. You could bet your buttons, things would go easy for Polly Dethier.

Clothilde finished the clams. She covered the bowl with a plate, to keep flies out, and scooped the shells and skins into a bucket, to take them down to the beach. Looking out the window, she saw Mother, just standing beside the garden. Mother wore a big hat and white gloves, and she was holding an empty basket. She stood still, studying the garden, with the slim skirt of her white dress moving in the breeze. Where had she gotten those gloves from, where had she had them packed away? And why was she just standing there, when the garden needed weeding? Clothilde watched her mother, the straight back and small waist, the gloved hand resting on top of her hat as if the breeze wanted to take it away when barely any breeze blew.

She knew Lou was right—something was wrong with Mother. But there was nothing she could do. There was never anything she could do. Except wish her father hadn't come back.

"I used to think," Lou's voice called her attention, "if I was an orphan—especially when my pa goes after me."

But Lou's father was a bad man—even with the new law prohibiting liquor, Lou's father managed to go on getting drunk because he had found a job on boats smuggling illegal whiskey down from Canada. Except for the smuggling job, Lou's father didn't keep any work he got. He'd moved to Maine when he was through working in the Rhode Island mills; he lived as a coastal for a season, gathering up whatever debris floated down from the lumber camps, and lumber mills, selling it wherever he could. Then he moved into the village, rented a two-room lean-to behind the blacksmith's stable, and hired his sons out to lobstermen and fishermen when they needed an extra hand, taking their wages himself. Lou, he had brought with him, that first day when he came out to ask Mother if she needed a man to work the fields. "She's strong and she's obedient," he'd said. Lou hadn't said anything. "And she's honest," he'd added, as if Mother might be wondering about that.

"I don't know that being an orphan is so bad," Lou said.

What did Lou think, if she thought she could feel sorry for Clothilde, and Mother? Clothilde couldn't stand people feeling sorry for her. She didn't want anybody's pity. Especially a servant's.

She didn't say a word to Lou, didn't even show she'd heard the words. She picked up the bucket by its steel handle and went out, through the ell. If there were going to be wars, she thought, going outside onto the grassy yard, then it should be different. If God wanted there to be wars, and men wanted to kill people and conquer other countries—it wasn't just men who got hurt, either, it was people who had nothing to do with it, women and children, old people, sick people—Edith Cavell, she had been a nurse and they shot her, and they dropped bombs on the city of London where all kinds of people lived, not just soldiers—and there were French farms and towns that got used as battlefields. . . .

If she were God, Clothilde thought, crossing the grass, she wouldn't have wars. Or, if there had to be wars, then the men would either get killed or not. There wouldn't be any wounded, there wouldn't be anybody like Jeb Twohey, it would be everything or it would be nothing. You'd die or you'd come back fine.

She went down the wooden steps to the beach, holding the railing carefully with one hand. She had read the newspapers the teacher brought to school. She could read through them, she had plenty of time at recesses—she could tell when someone was too stupid to see the truth of what he was describing, or when he was trying to hide the truth—and that showed what he was trying to hide. You couldn't trust what they said in the newspaper, she'd figured that out. Clothilde read the articles, and looked at the maps, and used her head, and she couldn't understand why God let anybody have a war.

She crossed the beach, walking out until she met the incoming tide. She lifted the bucket up and poured its contents back into the water.

The man in the boathouse had come back a week ago. He had walked up the driveway, with the sun behind him, so he was like a walking shadow, dark and featureless. He wore a short coat and his hat brim hid his face, and his bent head hid his face. He walked slowly, arms stiff. By the time he got to the front door, they had all gathered there, except Lou, because Lou spent Sunday nights in the village with her family.

It was last Sunday, the Sabbath, when the man returned. He stood there with his head down, so all they could see was the top of his broad hat. Then he lifted his face to let them see him.

Dierdre cried out, and cried for Mother. She ran to hide behind Mother's skirts, and scream. Nate turned abruptly and went back into the house, and they didn't see him again that night. Clothilde just stood there.

The face had skin that was not like human skin, not smoothly fitted over its bones. The skin was red and lumped, like a statue made out of clay by a child who didn't know how to make anything. The far end of one eyelid drooped down, lumpy, white, and the face had no eyebrows.

The face had dark blue eyes, eyes that looked at them all, at the place where Nate had stood, and at Dierdre clutching at Mother's skirt, trying to climb up into Mother's arms, at

Clothilde. Mother bent down and took Dierdre into her arms. Dierdre, sobbing, hid her face in Mother's neck, and her hands clutched at Mother's shoulders. Mother had tears pouring down her cheeks, and she didn't say a word.

Clothilde wished she could run away, or hide her face and scream. Her pain and her anger—they burned in her until she thought if she had a gun she would shoot it at the face, and kill him.

The face had no expression. The mouth started to move.

"I'm sorry," he said, in Father's voice.

Sorry for what? Clothilde's mind asked, bitter, so bitter her mouth dried up around the question.

He stood there, his boots coated with dust and mud, as if he'd walked all the way from France, all the years. "I'm home."

3

In the evening, after Clothilde and Lou had made the chowder, they gathered together in the parlor where, as always, Mother read the Gospels to them. They had eaten a supper of thick toasted bread, spread with butter and sprinkled with cinnamon and sugar. After the meal, while Mother gave Dierdre her bath, Lou washed the few dishes and Clothilde chopped onions and potatoes. Now the chowder was simmering on the stove and they were all sitting around the parlor while Mother read.

Lou and Clothilde had handiwork to do, but Nate sat motionless. He was too old to whittle the way he had when he was younger. Dierdre sat on the rug with the cloth doll Mother had made for her. Lou darned stockings, mostly Clothilde's because she seemed to get more tears in hers than anyone else. Lou's black thread wove back and forth, over and under, mending the tear. Clothilde had been given Father's opera cloak to carefully unmake, separating the white silk lining from the fine-woven black wool. She would have the black, for a dress if there was enough material, or a skirt. Dierdre would have the lining for a party dress, if there should be a party for her to go to, where a white silk dress would be the proper thing to wear.

Clothilde cut through the tiny stitches, one by one, with the little sharp tool Mother had for ripping out hems. Nate sat on the sofa beside Mother, leaning forward, his elbows on his knees, his chin on his elbows, his eyes on the floor.

Mother read in a smooth, light voice. When she read from the Bible it was a slower speech than when she talked because her mouth formed the syllables more carefully. She read Acts. How many times in her twelve years she had heard this, Clothilde couldn't have said. Between Mother's nightly readings and church on Sundays, many times. "For as I passed by, and beheld your devotions, I found an altar with this inscription, TO THE UNKNOWN GOD. Whom therefore ye ignorantly worship, Him declare I unto you," Mother read. She didn't read dramatically, with a voice that rose and fell, making the words important. Mother read quietly.

Clothilde's hand worked along the seams of the voluminous cloak. She had removed the frogs that closed the neck and now she was taking off the collar piece. The tiny stitches came close together, and she bent over the work, with the light from the gas lamp illuminating each stitch. One after the other, with no discernible difference between them, the stitches waited. She severed them, each one. When she had a few inches done, she went back to pick out the threads. Her mind wandered off from the reading.

They didn't even know for sure about God, that was what the Bible was saying. There were people who said, and the minister had made sermons on the subject, that the war was foretold in Revelations, that the stars falling like figs were like the bombs falling, that the Anti-Christ was a symbol for the Germans and Austrians, that the four horsemen, who rode ahead of the Apocalypse itself, had been seen, riding across Europe. Clothilde almost hoped they were right, because then you could understand what God was up to.

When Father had told them he was going away to war, it was at Grandfather's dinner table. Though dinner in Maine was eaten at the kitchen table, dinner at Grandfather's had always been a formal meal. Only on Sunday night did Nate and Clothilde and Mother eat with Father's family. So it must have been a Sunday.

At Grandfather's, the table was covered with white linen, and the heavy silver was set out at each place, forks on the left, knife and spoons on the right. The servants didn't sit down with them, of course. Harkness and May waited on table, serving the food Mrs. Oxford had cooked. There was a lot of food, so if you wanted dessert you had to eat lightly of the other courses, the soup, the roast, the dishes of potatoes and vegetables Harkness and May carried around the table, offering servings. Grandfather sat at one end of the table and carved. Aunt Leona sat at the other because she was the oldest woman, so she was the hostess. Father and Aunt Nora sat across from Mother, who had Nate on one side of her and Clothilde on the other. Clothilde remembered.

"I've enlisted," Father announced. In his white dress shirt and dark evening jacket, he was handsome. When he was happy, his dark blue eyes shone. They shone then, under the long golden lashes.

"Why do a fool thing like that?" Grandfather said.

The aunts murmured, "Oh, Benjamin," almost in unison, as if Father was Clothilde's age and had been caught with his fingers in one of Mrs. Oxford's puddings. Mother didn't say anything. She sat there as if she were nothing more than a painting, a portrait of a woman in a red-and-silver striped dress. "I asked you a question," Grandfather said.

"Well, sir, you know how everybody says *C'est la guerre*—this is my chance to find out what that means," Father said. That was a joke, his smiling face said. Nobody smiled back at him.

For a long time, nobody said anything. From where she sat, Clothilde could see Harkness make a face at May, the same kind of face Nurse made at Clothilde to warn her to be silent. The aunts waited for what Grandfather would say. Mother twisted her napkin in her hands. Clothilde couldn't see Nate, but she guessed he must be proud. Father would make a fine soldier, she thought. He should be a captain, because he was so strong and brave. There wasn't anyone who took fences as boldly as Father, and he was always there at the kill, when the fox was finally run to earth. She would have liked to say something, but she knew what would happen if she did. Children, as Nurse told them, were to be seen and not heard.

Grandfather picked up his knife and fork again. He cut a bite of roast and chewed on it. He stared at Father, who leaned back and smiled. Grandfather took a drink of wine, still staring, and Father, who wasn't afraid of Grandfather, smiled right back.

But Grandfather was angry. He was always cross at Clothilde and Nate and Mother, but this was more. He picked up his fork and ate a carrot, chewed and swallowed it. His gray eyes were always cold, like a November sky, but this was more, this was like ice on a frozen pond. Grandfather ate a roasted potato. He drank a sip of wine. He ate a tiny white onion, chewed it, and swallowed. He stared at Father and Father smiled. The only sound was the sound of Grandfather's fork and knife, clinking on the china plate.

"You know how I feel about you joining up," Grandfather finally said. His thick gray eyebrows lowered when he was angry. They were low now. "One assumes that, not having completed your college education, the army doesn't care to make you an officer."

"It's the cavalry, actually, sir," Father answered. He sounded as if he thought Grandfather was funny. "I'm taking Bucephalus."

Grandfather's eyebrows sank lower still, and gathered themselves together over the bridge of his nose. "Are you informing me that you are going to give over to the army a horse for which I paid one thousand dollars? To be used as a battle mount? Do you mean to sit there and tell me that, as if it were something humorous?"

"He's intelligent and he trusts me absolutely. He's the best choice. A horse like that—he may well save my life, sir." As if he knew what Grandfather would say to that, Father went on. "You did give him to me."

"I don't give gifts so they can be thrown away," Grandfather said. "A fine hunter which can later be used to breed colts that others will be eager to own—that's not the proper use of a good investment, giving it to the army."

"Cavalry," Father corrected.

Grandfather was eating, but only the aunts joined him. Mother sat twisting her napkin. Grandfather knew everyone was waiting for him to speak, so they would know what to say, but he chewed and thought. Clothilde wondered if he could make Father stay home, or tell him he had to take another horse. Bucephalus was big and dark, muscular and wild-looking, like a real war horse.

Grandfather patted his mouth with his napkin, then placed it neatly beside his plate, to show he was finished eating. "What plans have you made for your family, Benjamin?" he asked.

Father hadn't expected that question, and neither had Mother, whose fingers stopped moving.

"My family will remain here while I'm away," Father said. "This is my home."

"This is *my* home," Grandfather corrected him. "As long as you are living here, it is your home too." He gave Father a minute to think about that. Now Grandfather was smiling. "If you leave home, I'm going to ask you to take your family with you."

"Don't you think you're being unreasonable?" Father asked Grandfather.

Grandfather picked up his wine glass. The facets of the cut glass caught at the candlelights, flashing different colors, glassy red, glassy yellow, glassy green. Grandfather's hand turned the glass around. "No, I don't. In fact, I think I've been more than reasonable. Other men, if their sons, their only sons, ran off to marry some unsuitable woman, might refuse to have the woman or her children in the house. Other fathers might disown their sons. No, Benjamin, I don't think you can tell me I'm unreasonable."

Father didn't try to argue. "We'll rent a house then, perhaps in Boston. My family can live there while I'm away."

"Live on what?" Grandfather asked, so pleasantly that it worried Clothilde.

"There's my share of the income from the trust fund that Mother left to her children," Father reminded Grandfather.

"I'm afraid that, as the only executor of that trust, I cannot permit the money to be used in that fashion. As sole executor, my decision would be that while you are away from home, and in no need of the money, all income should be held in the bank, earning interest, to await your return."

Aunt Leona smiled at Aunt Nora when Grandfather said that. Clothilde, looking at them, saw it. It was just a little smile, and Aunt Nora smiled a little cat smile back. They didn't say anything. This was men's business, and this was Grandfather's house.

"I'll support my family by what I am paid, then," Father said.

Clothilde didn't know her father could earn money.

Grandfather, however, had another idea about it. "Do you have any idea what an ordinary cavalryman earns, Benjamin? I imagine you didn't even inquire. If you hadn't been asked to leave Yale College, of course, you might well have been made an officer. Perhaps then your family would have been able to live on what you earned, but as things are. . . ."

When Father was angry his cheeks got red and his neck stiff. Clothilde watched his cheeks flush and his neck, above the starched white collar, stiffen. But he always sounded as if things didn't matter, as if everything was a game. "You have a long memory, Father. It must be a source of great comfort to you. But I do wish that you could also remember what happens when you try to force me to do your bidding."

Grandfather put his glass back on the table. He wanted to say something, but he didn't. His gray eyebrows drew together.

"In that case," Father said, "the best thing is for my family to go to Maine, to Clothilde's property. They'll live at Speer Point."

Clothilde hadn't known she had property, and she wasn't sure what property was but she was glad if it helped Father beat Grandfather. She looked across Mother to try to catch Nate's eye, but Nate was staring at his plate.

"Your aunt's house burned to the ground," Grandfather said. "You know that."

Father wasn't worried. "There's a farmhouse, where the caretaker lived."

"You'll put your family into a farmhouse?" Grandfather asked. Clothilde wondered what was so bad about a farmhouse that she didn't know about. "You'd do better to send them back to that nuns' orphanage where your wife came from."

But the orphanage was only for girls, and what would Nate do? The orphanage was for orphans.

"I will take care of my family," Father repeated. "We'll all be leaving your home."

Clothilde didn't know where they were going. She'd never lived anywhere else.

"And the factory?" Grandfather asked.

"As I told you," Father said, smiling again, his blue eyes laughing at Grandfather. He knew he'd won. Clothilde had, somehow, helped him win, and she didn't know now if she was glad or not. "My country is at war, and I have a duty to fulfill."

Now Clothilde understood. Father didn't want the factory, Grandfather's factory, which manufactured carriages. It used to make carriages for horses to pull but Grandfather had changed it so it now made carriages for electric automobiles. Nate sometimes pointed an automobile out to her and told her that it had a Speer carriage, made in Grandfather's factory. It made Grandfather angry that Father didn't want his factory, wasn't interested in it, wouldn't go there to work. By going to war, Father was getting away from the factory.

"You expect me to be proud of you," Grandfather said.

"No, sir, I don't," Father answered.

That evening was the last time they had dinner with Grandfather. Harkness and May looked swollen up with the news they'd overheard, as they cleared the dinner plates and served Mrs. Oxford's strawberry fool for dessert. Clothilde wasn't hungry for dessert that night, not even for strawberry fool.

It took only three days to pack up their rooms and clothing. The furniture was all Grandfather's, so they didn't have to worry about that. Father was away most of the day and every evening, saying good-bye to his friends, so Mother did the packing. No servant came to help. Clothilde and Nate did what they could, but they mostly just stood watching, talking quietly as Mother filled trunks. "They were always mean," Nate whispered. He meant the aunts, and Grandfather, because of the way they made Mother stay alone in her own parlor while their friends came to see them in their big parlor. "When I grow up," Nate whispered, "I'm going to have a fine house, for Mother to live in, and servants who will do what she says. She'll have friends, too."

Clothilde thought that sounded fine. She knew Nate

could do that, because everyone liked Nate. "What's wrong with being Catholic?" she asked.

Nate shook his head. Two years older, and a boy, he knew much more than she did. "You're too young to understand," he said.

Mother let the heavy lid of the trunk fall down. She bent to pull the leather straps up around it.

"She comes to church with us," Clothilde insisted.

"That doesn't make any difference," Nate told her.

Clothilde thought that if she could understand then she wouldn't be so worried. She wanted to know what Mother had done so wrong that Grandfather never liked her. If she understood, then she'd know why the nursery and her bedroom were no longer hers, and she'd know why the aunts, who used to pretend that they were being polite, no longer even pretended. She did understand that her aunts were ashamed because Mother was an orphan raised by nuns. At first, Clothilde thought that her aunts just didn't like orphans, but then they kept knitting booties and blankets and sweaters for the poor Belgian orphans; all of the ladies did that in the afternoons in Grandfather's parlor, all except Mother. Clothilde decided then that the aunts didn't want an orphan actually living with them, and she knew they didn't want any orphan's children. She wanted to understand because whatever it was that Mother had done wrong, Clothilde had done it too.

Father's clothes took four trunks, because he often had to dine at his friends' houses or with his father, or go out in the mornings to his club. Mother and Nate and Clothilde used to like to stand at the window of the parlor, to watch Father ride off. He wouldn't ever go in the carriage with Grandfather and the aunts, or in the electric automobile, not even when he was dressed in his finest evening clothes, the long cloak hanging from his shoulders. Mother only needed two fine dresses, a green silk and a red silk with the narrow skirts that fashionable ladies were wearing. She wore the red silk on Christmas Day and the green on New Year's Day. Mother only needed one trunk.

Standing and watching, because there wasn't much a girl of eight could do, Clothilde felt the oriental rug under her feet and the polished wood floor under that. Under that, she knew, were huge wooden beams, running across the ceiling of the cellars, holding up the floor. She was afraid, but she didn't say anything. She was afraid because it felt like the rug and boards and beams were all falling away from under her feet. She felt like she was about to fall too.

She didn't know where they were going. She had always lived in Grandfather's house, and now they were being sent away from it. Father was sending them away, and Grandfather was, and everybody was glad they were going. Everybody except Mother and Nate and her. The aunts and the servants agreed with Grandfather; they didn't think Mother could take care of her and Nate.

Early one morning, they all stood at the door to watch Father ride off, ride away on Bucephalus. Later that same morning, Mother and Nate and Clothilde got into a carriage driven by Harkness, but nobody stood at the door to see them go. Their trunks traveled with them on the train.

At first, Mother sat in the parlor of the farmhouse on Speer Point, wearing a morning dress, for most of the day. She would have bread, eggs, milk, and butter delivered to the door, and she would cook meals for them. Clothilde and Nate explored outside when the weather permitted, but they stayed close to the house because there were no streets to guide them home if they went too far. Mostly, they went down to the beach. Then Father arrived unexpectedly that one afternoon, wearing his uniform. He gave Mother a purse full of money. "I sold everything I could, Marie. You should have more than enough to see you through. You'll have to take care of things, while I'm gone. Marie? You're going to have to run the household." Mother promised she would. "This war won't last much longer, now we're in it," he told Mother. "Clothilde, why don't you smile? Haven't you got a smile for your handsome father?"

Clothilde shook her head. She wanted him to stay, but he left the next afternoon.

Father wrote to them, every week. The letter came on Monday or Tuesday. They would all walk into the village together, and Mrs. Twohey would give them their letter. Mother would read it to them, after supper, before she read the Bible. Father told them about his new friends and about Bucephalus, what Bucephalus was learning to do and how clever and brave the horse was. Father sometimes drew a picture, to show them what it looked like at the training camp, or how they played cards at night. He always put a postscript at the end of his letters, saying, "Tell Clothilde to smile."

It made Clothilde smile the way he always said that. She tried not to, but she smiled anyway.

It was after Father rode away that last time that Mother started to work, cutting branches off the old apple trees in the small orchard, and wearing not her laced shoes but a pair of Father's old hacking boots. She told them all about the flower garden she wanted to grow, around at the front of the house where the plants would be protected from the sea winds. After Father had gone, Mother agreed to let Mr. Small work the fields, and to have Lou as their servant. She made Nate clean off and oil the rusty tools they found hanging neatly in the barn. Instead of flowers, she planted onions, potatoes, and vegetables in the garden Tom Hatch turned over for them. "When Father returns, there will be time for flowers," she said. "When Father returns, we'll have a home for him."

"But it's mine," Clothilde reminded her.

Mother just shushed her, saying she was only a child.

All that summer, after Mr. Small had been sent away and Lou moved into her room in the ell, they learned how to do things, how to dig for clams, how to weed and sew and sail the skiff that Tom Hatch brought around from the old boathouse for them. They learned how to feed coal into the boiler, so there would be hot water for the house. Mother had money for seeds, for coal, for flour and meat. Mother had money to hire people to help, if she needed it, but she wanted to save as much as she could. Mother already knew how to cook, because the nuns had taught her. Mother could make the simplest meals taste good.

Mother wrote to Father about all the things they were doing, and he wrote back or drew sketches of what he was doing. When Dierdre was born, with Lou's help because Lou had helped her own mother have babies, she wrote to Father about that. By then, it was deep winter and Father's letters came from Europe, and were shorter. In March they had a letter that was just a drawing. The drawing showed Bucephalus, just his head but you could see he was lying flat on the ground, in mud, and he was hurt. A hand held a gun pointing beside his eye and they knew it was Father's hand. That letter didn't have any postscript.

After that, there were no letters, even though Mother walked to the village every day, despite the mud, and the black flies. It wasn't until summer that Grandfather wrote to say that Father was in a hospital and he might not ever come back. "He doesn't wish to communicate with you. You see what this marriage brought him to," Grandfather's letter said. Nate, who could read best, was reading the letter aloud.

Mother held Dierdre in her arms and just stared at the letter in Nate's hands. Dierdre had eyes that were dark blue like Father's; she reached up toward Mother's face, and laughed. After a while, Mother smiled back at Dierdre and then at the rest of them.

"But, ma'am," Lou said. "I thought they wrote to the wife, direct, the army. Can that man be blaming you for this war?"

"He'd like to," Mother said.

They didn't hear anything after that. When everybody else in the village celebrated the Armistice, the family on Speer Point was glad that finally the war was over, but they didn't feel like celebrating.

Grandfather wrote again in the spring. Clothilde hoped he was writing to tell them news of Father, but after that letter she made up her mind never to hope for anything again. Grandfather wanted Nate to live with him, and go to Phillips Academy, because now Nate would need to learn how to run the factory.

"Does that mean Father is dead?" Clothilde asked Nate, when Mother couldn't hear.

"He doesn't say. Probably."

Clothilde didn't want Nate to go, but Mother said that he should. "If the factory is mine," Nate argued, "then I can bring you and Mother and Dierdre to live with me, and take proper care of you."

Clothilde shook her head. She didn't say anything, she couldn't because she had that feeling again, of trying to stand on something that wasn't there.

"Don't you want to get away from here?" Nate asked her.

Clothilde shook her head. She wanted Nate to stay.

"You'll see," Nate said. "You'll see. I've got it all worked out. I hate him too, I'll write you lots of letters, I'll take care of you all."

Clothilde didn't know who to hate.

As it turned out, Nate didn't write often from school, because he was too busy. He stayed at Grandfather's over long vacations, because there were fellows who wanted him to visit them, and at Phillips Academy he lived in a dormitory. Grandfather wanted him to stay for the summer, too, but Nate told him he was going home for the summer. Clothilde almost hoped then that things would get back to normal, but it was a good thing she didn't because when Nate arrived, and unpacked his two trunks of new clothes, it turned out that one thing he was looking forward to at home was seeing his new friends, who had summer cottages in the town across the bay.

Nate hadn't even been home a month when the man walked up their driveway. The man stayed for only one meal. Nate had left the house and Dierdre wouldn't come out of the parlor, so it was just the three of them at the table. The man spooned up his chowder awkwardly. His hand clutched the spoon. Clothilde watched until it got about as far up as his neck.

All anyone said during the meal was when the man's voice announced that he wasn't going to sleep in this house. Clothilde waited for Mother to say something, but Mother was silent. "There's a boathouse," Clothilde finally told him, her eyes staying at the shoulders of the worn coat. She had eaten all of her bowl of chowder only because on Sundays she washed up dishes, because Lou went to evening service and spent the night with her family. The chowder had no flavor and she didn't know why she had eaten it all. She didn't know why she had told him about the boathouse, and she wished he would go away. She had gotten used to the idea that he'd never come home again, but now he was back.

After he'd left, Mother went to the door to watch him walk away and Clothilde had started to wash their few dishes. It scared her. He scared her, and Mother not saying anything scared her. Everything kept on hurting her. That was seven days ago, and Clothilde still didn't know how to make herself safe.

4

THE next day was Sunday, so Clothilde, Nate, and Mother went to the morning services. The day was clear, bright, and windless, a good walking day. By the time they returned, Lou and Dierdre had the table set and the chowder heated. The chowder Lou and Clothilde made wasn't as good as Mother's, thinner, somehow, the clams not as swollen up with sweetness; Lou didn't make the little crisp chunks of salt pork to scatter over the top. Lou's biscuits were not as light as Mother's and their taste was somehow flat. At the table, Mother sat quiet, letting Clothilde and Nate heap as much jam as they wanted onto their biscuits. Dierdre was talking away, telling them about the church service her doll went to, but nobody paid any attention. Clothilde counted: it was seven days since the man in the boathouse had walked up to their door; it was twenty-three days since the carriage had brought Nate home; how many days was it since Mother had prepared a meal, worked in the vegetable garden, scolded her?

"Dolly Molly wasn't listening nicely," Dierdre reported. "I had to shush—"

Nate interrupted. "I've been invited to go on a cruise," he said. He didn't look at anyone when he said that. "A boy

38

from school, his people live in Chicago, they have one of
the summer places. They'll be sailing down to Fisher's
Island, and back, and they've asked me along."

Clothilde stopped eating.

Nate waited for Mother to give him permission. He
looked handsome and healthy, sitting there waiting. He
looked like a young gentleman. He had grown up at school
that year, and his brown hair lay smooth on his head, parted
in the middle. He didn't look like the Nate she remembered,
who had played endless games of cribbage with her on the
long winter days and nights, until he owed her hundreds of
dollars. Clothilde had luck with cards, he said, sometimes
laughing at her, sometimes cross. Sometimes Nate won a
game, but not often—he missed seeing fifteens in a hand, or
he'd play out his cards without trying to guess what was in
her hand so he could win an extra point or two. Nate used
to joke that, if she were a man, Clothilde could support the
family by gambling. Sometimes Clothilde would like her
brother so much, his easygoing good humor and his
handsomeness, that she would play out her hand without
claiming all the points she could have gotten from it. Nate
never knew when she did that, never noticed; he'd just be
glad he was winning. When he went away to school, Nate
learned a game called bridge, which took four players so he
couldn't teach it to her.

Clothilde knew things looked different to Nate, after the
year away, but she had thought he wanted to be home with
them for the summer. She had thought he would stay home
for the whole long summer.

She looked around the big table. The pine shone golden
and the utensils were steel, but it was beginning to feel like
the table in Grandfather's house. Mother ate small, unhun-
gry mouthfuls. Lou sat with Dierdre beside her, watching
Dierdre's manners to be sure she mopped her mouth and
spooned up her chowder neatly. Lou buttered Dierdre's
biscuits, giving her a half at a time, not letting her have any

jam until she'd cleaned her bowl. While Nate waited for
Mother to answer his request, Dierdre said, "I can go too."

Mother ignored Dierdre, just as the aunts would have, so
it was Lou who shushed her.

"Do I have your permission to go?" Nate asked, not
looking at any of them.

Clothilde didn't think he should be allowed. He'd been
gone all year. At first, the first few days, he'd said he was
glad to be back, especially glad to be away from the Old
Man, which was what Nate now called Grandfather.

"You know that I can't give permission," Mother said.

"Why not?" Clothilde asked. If Mother couldn't, who
could?

"This doesn't concern you, Clothilde," Mother said. She
didn't sound cross, she didn't sound anything. She brushed
Clothilde away as if Clothilde were a fly. Everything was
calm with Mother these days. She didn't hurry, she didn't
dawdle, her voice was always the same smooth voice and
her face was always the same smooth arrangement. Even if
she was an orphan, Mother knew how a lady acted. "We'll
have to see what your father says," Mother said.

"I can ride a boat," Dierdre said. "I'm pretty. I want to
go."

"Hush," Lou told her, moving Dierdre's cup of milk out
of reach of her waving arms.

Dierdre gave Mother an earnest, begging look. Clothilde
thought that her sister probably really did think she had a
chance to go with Nate. Thinking she had a chance made
Dierdre want it even more.

"You weren't invited, Dierdre," Clothilde explained.

"I have too," Dierdre said. "Did too."

She could probably tell them when, too, and what Dolly
Molly said about it.

"Will you ask permission for me?" Nate asked Mother.

Mother shook her head. "I can't. He doesn't want to see
anybody."

"But—" Nate started to protest. Then he leaned back in his chair and smiled around at all of them. "They're leaving tomorrow. I won't need anything I don't have, there's no difficulty about clothing, just the one suitcase."

"Me too," Dierdre said, leaning back, smiling around.

Nate leaned over to put his big hand under her chin. "Ladies don't go on long cruises," he said gently to her. "It's only men who go. The life isn't nice enough for ladies."

This was the Nate Clothilde couldn't look at without her heart feeling soft and her smile spreading over her face, the Nate who could say no to Dierdre by giving her a reason she would like.

"I'm a lady," Dierdre told him. "I'm going to have a party dress."

"You're a fine lady," Nate agreed, then smiled at Mother: "I guess I'm going to go, so you might as well give me your permission."

Clothilde waited for Mother to lose her temper. But Mother's mouth didn't purse out, the way it did when she was getting angry at one or the other of them for being saucy. Mother's mouth stayed in the same pretty little smile, not really a smile so much as a pleasant expression, like a doll's painted face."

Clothilde knew then that Nate would be going.

"Grandfather would like to hear that you were making the right sort of friends," Mother said. She said that as if it were important. "You must do what you think best," she said.

"She means no, Nate," Clothilde told her brother. "That's what she means, and you know it."

"There's no need to shriek, Clothilde," Mother said.

"I'm not shrieking," Clothilde answered back. Mother didn't say a word. "He shouldn't go. He's always going away." But she couldn't make Mother hear her words. Mother just shook her head calmly.

"He's nearly a man grown, dear."

"I know, but—" Clothilde wanted to say all the things she'd been thinking about Nate and what was different, how he'd changed, but one look at Mother's face told her it wouldn't be any good. Mother wasn't even really looking at her. Clothilde gave up. It was no use. Mother's behavior was because of the man in the boathouse, somehow, but knowing that didn't help Clothilde any. She couldn't count on Nate anymore, and she'd learned that, learned to do without him. She couldn't count on Mother, either, she guessed. She couldn't imagine this woman climbing up to prune old overgrown limbs from apple trees, sawing until sweat stained her armpits; she couldn't imagine her calling down to them sharply to stand clear and then hurry in to drag the branches to the brush pile; this woman couldn't have sent Lou's father packing. Clothilde looked at Lou's worried face.

"Me too, I'm going with Nate," Dierdre announced. "Grandfather says," she said.

Fury burst up inside Clothilde. "You can't go, didn't you hear them?" she asked. She knew she shouldn't be so angry at Dierdre, who was still a baby, but she couldn't stop herself. "You don't know anything."

"Do too," Dierdre said.

"You're a baby," Clothilde reminded her.

"Am not," Dierdre denied it, and burst into baby tears. "Am not! Am not!" she cried, and splashed both hands into her bowl of chowder.

"I don't know why you can't control these children, Lou," Mother said. She rose from the table, drawing her long skirt back as if she didn't want it near them. At the kitchen door she turned around. "You know I can't listen to this—fighting," she said to all of them. She went calmly into the parlor.

Clothilde got up to take the bowls from the table. Lou had a cloth and was mopping up Dierdre's mess. Nate just sat there.

"I didn't have a biscuit," Dierdre protested, as Clothilde took away her bowl. "I want a biscuit and I want jam." Clothilde let her scream and cry. Lou didn't say anything. Nate just sat there, like the king of Persia, waiting for the table to be cleared.

Clothilde stood beside him, with her hands on her hips. "Nobody all of a sudden goes off on a cruise."

"You don't know anything about it," Nate said.

"You're just running away," she told him, wanting him to deny it.

"From what?" he asked, smiling up at her. "If you're so all-fired smart." His eyes smiled too, gray-blue and distant, as if he knew things she didn't.

"From—you know—from him."

"Clothilde, you're such a child. You don't know anything."

"Anyway," Clothilde switched back to the point, "people don't."

"You don't know anything about that, either. You're just jealous, because nobody invites you."

"I am not."

"All right. All right. Take it easy."

"Why would I be jealous?"

Nate leaned his elbows on the table and just grinned at her. Because he was a boy, Clothilde thought, and could fight, and got sent away to a school. Because he could run away, he had friends to run away to. "Well I'm not," she said, and wanted it to be the truth. "Not a bit."

"Me too," Dierdre said, coming to stand with her little hands balled up into fists, on Nate's other side. She was so short and so positive and made so little sense, that both Nate and Clothilde burst out laughing. Laughing with her brother, Clothilde wished he weren't going to go away again. She wished he wanted to stay home.

She looked up then and saw Mother standing in the doorway. "Aren't you the silly ones," Mother said. Mother had dressed her hair for church, and it puffed away from her face in smooth, light brown billows. Her eyes, blue as a June sky, looked serious, but her lips smiled, as if she didn't mind them being silly. Clothilde studied her mother, tall for a woman and with the narrow waist that was part of a woman's beauty, her skirt hanging smoothly to just above her dainty ankles. "If you would all come to the parlor? I need to talk with you," Mother said. "You as well, Louisa, the dishes will have to wait."

Lou dried her hands on the apron, then took it off and hung it on its peg beside the sink. There was something in Mother's voice that said this was not the time to wear an apron. When Lou got to the parlor, she didn't sit down. Instead, she stood by the door, the way the servants in Grandfather's house did, the way Mother had asked her to before they all got used to working together and sitting down together. Mother put Dierdre on her lap, holding the chubby ankles still with a hand so Dierdre wouldn't kick. Clothilde sat on one of the two black chairs that matched the sofa where Mother sat. She put her feet neatly together and folded her hands in her lap. She sat up straight. She didn't know why she was afraid of what Mother was going to say.

"I've been told that we are facing some difficulties," Mother said. "Something to do with money. I'm sure that when he is better, Father will take care of them, but until that time—"

"What do you mean better?" Nate interrupted.

"Don't interrupt, Nathaniel."

"He's been sent back," Nate pointed out, "so they think he's better already. This *is* better."

Mother ignored him. "There is difficulty about money. I don't understand it," she went on, as if it didn't matter that she didn't understand, as if it was right that she shouldn't. "As a consequence, however, we will have to practice economies."

But why was Mother saying she didn't understand, when

it had been she who had overseen everything in all the years they had been living here? It was Mother who ordered food and paid the money owing to Mr. Grindle, who had determined and paid out Lou's wages. It was Mother who had hired Tom Hatch to turn over the ground for the vegetable garden, who had brought the apple trees back to fruitfulness. It was Mother who had run the household, overseeing the meals and cleaning, the washing and mending, the schoolwork, who had chased after them to do their chores properly. Why did she now claim not to understand? Clothilde didn't understand.

"What about the check from the army that comes every month?" she asked.

Mother shook her head. "Now that he's back that won't be sent. So that, among other economies, we can no longer offer you employment, Louisa. I want to express my gratitude to you, for your years of service. I am sorry to have to let you go."

What they would do without Lou, Clothilde couldn't think. She didn't know how to stop what Mother was doing.

"Please, Mrs. Speer," Lou asked. Her face was even paler than usual. "Who will do my chores?"

Lou didn't want to leave them, any more than Clothilde wanted her to go.

"Clothilde will," Mother said.

But how could she go to school and still do all of Lou's work? And, if she didn't go to school, how could she go to a college and be able to find employment when she grew up? What would her future be? The questions rose up in Clothilde's mind, like waves under a stormy wind, but when she spoke her voice was small, and weak. "I'm supposed to go to school," she said.

Mother shook her head, No.

"But can't you do Lou's work? Or some of it," Clothilde pleaded. She could do more than she had, she thought, she just couldn't do all of it.

"Father wouldn't want his wife doing household chores," Mother said, as if that was something there could be no question about. But that made no sense. Hadn't Mother been his wife before, and done the work? Even if he wasn't there, she was still his wife. Did the man in the boathouse want his daughter to do it even though he wouldn't want his wife to? Was Clothilde supposed to become a servant so that Mother could be a lady?

She couldn't think, couldn't answer the questions, couldn't imagine—she could only sit there with her feet neatly side by side and be afraid.

"But Mrs. Speer, ma'am? I could stay on without the wages," Lou said.

"We couldn't ask that of you, Louisa. How would your family manage?"

"I can't go back and live there, ma'am. When he has money, he—" She looked at Clothilde for help, but Clothilde couldn't give her any. Lou was afraid to go live at home, Clothilde thought. She remembered bruises she had seen on Lou's arms when Lou rolled up her sleeves to do the Monday washing, and a swelling once that Lou had said was a bad tooth. She thought of what Lou said about Mr. Small taking too much to drink, and sailing on the boats that smuggled in black market whiskey from Canada. Mr. Small had to be a bad man, because if he earned money on those boats, why didn't they move into a decent house, a house with room for the large family? Lou was trying not to cry.

"You shouldn't make Lou go," Clothilde told her mother.

"Don't be so selfish, dear," Mother said.

"Please, ma'am. He'll hire me out to one of the summer cottages, I know he will. I don't need wages, ma'am, just a room of my own and I don't eat much."

"It's not right for a family to keep servants without paying them," Mother said. "It's a shame on the family.

I'm sorry, Louisa. You'll have a good recommendation, of course."

"Nate?" He was just sitting there. Clothilde asked him, "Do something."

"Is this your idea, or—his?" Nate asked his mother.

"Your father leaves the domestic details to me," Mother answered, which didn't answer the question at all.

"Why are we so short of money when we have the income from Father's trust?" Nate asked.

"Grandfather has been taking care of that, while your father was away. Father says Grandfather has used that money to keep you, Nate, at Phillips Academy, and to clothe you properly for your position in life."

"That's not true," Nate said. "He told me—" Nate bit down on the words and fell silent again.

"Anything left over, Grandfather has invested into the factory, which is Father's inheritance after all. Father won't let us starve."

Dierdre had finally figured out what was happening. She squirmed off Mother's lap and ran across to throw her arms around Lou's legs. "Don't go away," she cried. "I'll cry," she said, starting to cry already. "I'll cry and cry."

"Please, ma'am," Lou said. "I could stay until September. Or just through this month."

Mother flapped her hands helplessly around in her lap. "No more than a week or two, then," she gave in. "People always give a week or two notice, so that's all right. There's no need for you children to be so upset. If need be, Father says, we can sell Speer Point."

Clothilde didn't want to believe her ears.

"Who would you sell it to?" Nate asked. "Has someone made an offer?"

"A lumber company would want it for timber," Mother explained.

"But you can't do that. It's mine," Clothilde protested. "It's mine and I won't let you."

"You're only a child," Mother answered, brushing her away.

Nate was more patient. "Look, Clothilde, if the Old Man's putting money into the factory—because, it's these cheap gasoline models, and that Henry Ford, don't you see? Electric is better—didn't President Wilson get an electric automobile? But we have to compete harder right now."

Clothilde looked, but she didn't see why she had to give up the peninsula. It was hers, even if she was a child. There was a will. "I won't let you," she repeated.

"You can't stop it, dear, not if Father decides it's best. He's your father. Little girls don't know anything about property, so their fathers take care of it. Don't you want to help your family?"

Clothilde shook her head, No. She wasn't saying no to Mother's question, but to everything, to Father being able to sell the Point, to not being able to stop him, to Lou going away and Nate going away, to not being able to do anything about any of it. "No," Clothilde said. She said it around the room to everyone, "No."

"Yes," Dierdre yelled back. "Yes. Yes."

Clothilde got up and left the room, ignoring Mother's voice. She went upstairs to her bedroom. She kept saying it inside her, No, No, No, as if by saying it she could keep things from happening. She heard her feet slamming down on the stairs and on the floorboards of her room, which she and Lou had painted that winter. She heard her feet hit the floor of her bedroom, but it felt like the floor was gone out from under her. Clothilde sat down at the little table that made a writing desk in her room, tucked in under the low slanting ceiling, with the window off to her right.

She wasn't crying and she didn't even want to cry. If she was a grown-up, if she was a boy, she'd show them, she wouldn't let them. She wished she were Nate and had friends to go stay with. She wished she were Dierdre who didn't understand. She wished—if she were God—

Outside, the light shone and the leaves hung motionless. Clothilde got up to close her window. She sat down again, and thought she'd never get up, she'd just sit there until she died. In the silence, silence from downstairs, silence from outside, there was a rattling, as if the window shook in its frame. As if the window were knocking.

But it was a knock on her door, which was repeated before Lou opened it and stood in the doorway. "I've been thinking," Lou said, not coming into the room. "I could he'p my ma, with better wages from one of the summer cottages. I'm fifteen, and your mother has paid my wages to me, not to him, so we've got a little set aside. And it's not like having to go back to the mills, Clothilde, it's not the worst it could be."

"I don't care," Clothilde said. She didn't get up, and as soon as Lou had closed the door behind her, she turned back to the wall.

5

T HE wall had been painted blue, years and years ago, in her great-aunt's time, a blue the color of a robin's egg. The wall angled down from the ceiling and then straightened out just at Clothilde's eye level. The paint was faded with time, and little cracks ran along it, like pencil lines, making a design she couldn't see the order of. Clothilde stared at the wall. The feelings—anger and fear and misery—which had carried her up the stairs and given her voice, dropped her. She was like some fish dropped by a wave onto a rock, a rock alone in the middle of the ocean. There was nothing she was going to be able to do about anything.

The window knocked again.

Clothilde turned her face to it, without curiosity. She wasn't looking at the window, or through it. She just turned her face to it. The frame of wood held flat glass in place; beyond the glass was a view of leaves and branches and sky, as unmoving as a picture. Clothilde turned her face to the wall again, leaned her elbows on the tabletop, and covered her ears with her hands as she stared at the cracks on the wall.

She should have known that the peninsula couldn't be hers. Children didn't own things, girls didn't, people like her family didn't. People like Grandfather owned things and could decide how to use them. She wished she'd known that all along, because then . . .

The sound the window made, making it again, was like the knock of a giant hand. If it were a hand, it would be huge and heavy . . . the sound was like such a hand making itself as gentle as possible. The sound of that knocking echoed in Clothilde's bedroom and sounded as if it must be rattling the whole side of the house. If it was a hand, knocking . . .

Clothilde opened the window. Nothing came in. She hadn't expected anything to come in. She had probably imagined the sound, too, even though she could still hear it. She was probably going crazy, hearing things that weren't real. If you were crazy, like Jeb Twohey, then people would take care of you and you'd never have to know anything. You'd just be crazy until you could die and be done with being frightened and helpless.

Clothilde left her room. There had been that knock and it had to be answered, so she went down the stairs and out the front door. Not that she wanted to go answer, not that she didn't want to, not that she'd decided to: she went to answer it. She walked to the vegetable garden, where the early peas were growing taller and the lettuces curled delicately in upon themselves. The knocking wasn't to be answered there, nor among the apple trees of the orchard. It was crazy, she was crazy, the knocking that filled her skull was driving her crazy.

As if she were being pushed from behind, Clothilde moved slowly along the rutted driveway, into the trees. No sound broke the stillness. She walked under the branches of trees, which seemed to wait, listening in the silence. She followed the dirt roadway up beside the fields where Mr. Henderson's crop of mixed timothy and alfalfa sprouted up through the ground in thin green blades. She kept her shoes on the dirt track, one foot following the other, when the road reentered the woods. There pines stood at attention and even the birches seemed to have halted, in midgesture, like girls photographed at a dance. When the road looped around to the right to go to the ruined cottage, Clothilde left it and went on through the woods to the headlands. She moved slowly, as if she were being pulled.

When she stepped out onto the headlands, the sky and sea spread out before her, reflecting each other. The tide was out, but even with the knocking at last silenced, the water lay dark and still at the foot of the heavy rockfalls. The sunny air spread out all around her. Clothilde stepped out onto a flat chunk of granite. Sunlight fell over her. Her shadow lay curled at her feet.

"Clothilde," the Voice named her. "Child."

But she was alone. Clothilde spun around to see who had spoken, her heart beating fast. She saw no one. She didn't expect to see anyone, because nobody could have a voice like that. It was a huge, rich voice, rich like Mother's chowder, rich with pungent clam broth and sweet silky milk, with soft chunks of bland potatoes and sharp bits of onions, rich with the springy, nutty clams and crisp slivers of fried salt pork. She recognized the Voice, which she had never heard before. Her heart beat with painful slowness.

"Child," the Voice said again, but not from the woods she peered into. She turned around to catch it, over the water. "Clothilde."

It was behind her and in front of her. It surrounded her. It weighed down on her from above and rose up under her feet. But it wasn't the Voice that was making her feel squeezed; it was scaredness squeezing at her. Oh, she was glad—gladness burst out of her the way it had when she first stood on the headlands and understood that the peninsula lying behind her was hers, her own. With the gladness, however, she was also remembering, knowing, all of the things she shouldn't have done—the meannesses in her heart and the way she'd wanted to take away Polly Dethier's ruffledy dress and her dimple; times she'd sat there and watched Lou or Mother work when she could have got up and helped; and the way she'd run away from things at school instead of standing to fight them. The remembering made her afraid.

Clothilde turned around, putting the water behind her. She ran as fast as she could. She held her skirt up so her legs could move freely. She ran among the trees and through the woods, not following any path, dodging and ducking. Leaves brushed at her face. Branches slapped at her body. When a root caught at her foot, she stumbled but she didn't fall. She ran on.

The Voice ran beside her.

Clothilde's blood beat in her ears and she gasped for breath. It hurt her feet, the way they were pounding down onto the ground. It hurt her chest, the way it tried to suck in air. But the Voice beside her ran like water, flowed beside her like water.

Clothilde couldn't get away. She halted, and rested her forehead against the white trunk of a birch until she had caught her breath and had stopped the sobbing she hadn't realized she'd been doing as she ran. Then she turned around to return to the headlands, rubbing at her eyes and nose. She was tired. She'd been as frightened as she could stand to be, more frightened than she could have imagined being, and now she was too exhausted and afraid to feel frightened. She walked back through the shady woods, with the dappled sunlight falling like rain. The Voice walked beside her.

Standing again on the rock, facing again over the water, Clothilde just waited. Her hands felt like they were trembling, so she put them behind her back. There, they held tightly each to the other, and her fingers wound together. Her back straight, her shoulders stiff, Clothilde held her head up. She made her head stay up.

It wasn't gone, she knew that.

"All right," she said out loud. Her voice sounded thin and high. "I'm listening," she squeaked out.

"Sit down," the Voice told her. "Let your body rest upon the rock." The Voice was trying to make itself as little as it could, which wasn't very little. Clothilde almost smiled, at how large small was to the Voice.

"No," she said, adding politely, "thank you."

She waited to hear what the Voice wanted from her. Maybe it was going to tell her she was about to die. Maybe this was what happened when you died, and she was already dead. She looked quickly down at herself, the blouse, rumpled now from the exertions of running, the blue skirt hanging, the toes of her shoes with their laces threading back and forth between the eyelets. She didn't think she was dead.

"I—" she started to say. But she didn't know what to say next and she thought she should have kept on waiting. Was she supposed to stand and wait? "What—" she tried next, which was no better.

"You called to me," the Voice said. "Knocking upon my door."

"No, I didn't," Clothilde said. "Did I?" Because the Voice must be right about everything. "Why are you saying that?"

The Voice smiled. It wasn't the way a grown-up smiled at something a child said, and it wasn't the way someone smiled when he heard something funny. It wasn't exactly the way the whole world smiled on a bright day, but that was the closest.

"I didn't," Clothilde repeated. She wasn't going to be forced into saying something that wasn't true.

"Sit down," the Voice told her. "Sit down upon this rock, and let your body rest."

That was what Clothilde wanted to do, anyway. She sat down abruptly, Indian fashion, carefully arranging her skirt over her legs. Once she was sitting, she wanted to be

standing again. She needed to move, she could feel that in
her legs; but she wanted to sit still and silent, with not even
the blood going around her body. This was more than
frightened. This was fear of something you were glad to be
afraid of. "What do you want me for?" she finally asked,
looking out to the east, over the spreading sky and water, as
if she could see the Voice.

"To be my people, to know the creatures of land and sea
and air, to know the leaf and to know the tree. To carry light
in your hand as you step from one season to the next, to
guard the light from darkness, guard the darkness from
the—" The Voice stopped, as if it saw the smile Clothilde
was hiding. Of course the Voice couldn't understand her
question—it was too large to know how small she was—she
understood that, but the smile rollicked along under her skin
and the most she could do was to conceal it.

"Yes," the Voice said. Then, "Yes?"

"I meant, what do you want me to do?"

"You called to me," the Voice said.

"Do you mean, what do I want you to do?" she asked, so
surprised that she didn't hear the disrespectful speech until
she had uttered it. "I'm sorry—I didn't think—I shouldn't
have even—it doesn't matter," she said. "I shouldn't have
disturbed you, if I did. I didn't mean to. It's not important."

"The leaf grows and the tree grows; it is important."

Clothilde knew then what was happening, and she was
ashamed. She knew why it had happened—because it was
more than she could bear. To bear meant to carry, and her
strength wasn't equal to the weight of what piled up on her.
Like an egg you pushed and pushed down on until its shell
gave way, and your hand's weight crushed the shell into the
yolk and white, her brain had given way. She retreated into
herself, to find her normal self again. Her crazy self—the
self that thought she could call out and be answered, and be
asked what she wanted—as if God had time—Clothilde was
frightened of herself. She'd never been frightened of herself

before, and that frightened her even more. And if the Voice might be real—which she half believed—which was the craziest thing about the whole—she felt her brain's shell cracking.

Clothilde jumped up, to stand on the rock with her hands on her hips and the sea before her and the trees behind her. Turning her face right up to face the sky, she called: "Why do you make wars, anyway?"

It rose up, a great black wave from the sea. It curled over her. She was there where the air was thick yellow and red, where the thick air smelled of things burning, and of mud. She was there with whistling explosions, with voices crying out like the minister's description of damned souls, souls damned to hell, and crying out. She was there under an icy rain, where a doomed silence wrapped voices around, silence like a bandage that courage bound around an incurable wound. She was there, where a black horse lay fallen in mud that streaked his face like tears, his mouth frothing blood, and a man had to put the gun to the horse's head, and shoot Bucephalus even though Father would have been happier to put the gun to his own head, and his hand shook as he pulled the exploding trigger. The black wave held her, then passed on.

"The design is mine; the embellishments are yours. I do not make wars; men do."

"I'm sorry," Clothilde said. She sat down again, even though she hadn't been told to. She kept her eyes closed, for fear of what she might see if she opened them. All she wanted now was to be left alone. "I'm sorry. Really. Really sorry."

The Voice knew sorrow too, and when it next spoke it sounded like a foghorn, warning through the shrouded night to ships that it could not see and that could not see it, warning of the deadly rocks waiting invisible under the dark water. "What would you have?" the Voice asked,

Clothilde, eyes squeezed shut and covered by her hands,

shook her head. If her mind had given way—poor Jeb Twohey, his mind caught in that black wave that wouldn't ever let go of him. Oh, she could understand what had happened to Jeb Twohey.

The Voice asked, "What would you mend?"

"The man in the boathouse." Clothilde mumbled the words into her hands, not wanting to answer the question, answering with the first thing that came into her mind, not knowing until she answered how that was the first thing. Even if she'd taken her hands away from her face she couldn't have opened her eyes. "I'd make him better."

The Voice didn't know who she meant.

"Benjamin Speer," Clothilde named him, and the Voice recognized the name.

"Yes," the Voice agreed.

"And Nate shouldn't go on that cruise, he shouldn't, I wouldn't let him," Clothilde said, the words rushing out now, "and Lou—" But if she thought about Lou, it was just selfishness to say that she'd let Lou stay and work for them. What Lou really needed, to make her life better, was to be kept safe from her father. "Mr. Small shouldn't be able to hurt her."

"Yes," the Voice agreed. "Yes."

Clothilde thought, in the darkness of her hands over her closed eyes. She didn't want to be greedy and she didn't want to be silly. She wanted to ask if she couldn't be prettier than Polly Dethier, and strong enough to fight off the boys' teasing at school. She didn't let herself ask for that. What if, like a fairy tale, she only had three wishes? She would have already used them up. "And my peninsula, Speer Point," she added hastily. "Speer Point is *mine*."

"No," the Voice said. Then it was gone.

Clothilde had opened her mouth to argue, to ask why not. She took her hands away from her eyes and looked around. The air filled with noises, and she knew she was alone again. She heard the waves, as the tide rose and a breeze rose, she heard gulls, birds in the woods behind her, and the buzzing of insects.

The craziness had passed, like a fit of laughter or tears. She was almost sorry, then. She was almost glad. She was entirely confused, except for the solid rock underneath her. She turned around, putting her hand down on the sharp rock, looking all around her.

It was more than any eye could take in all at once. The pines growing straight up, each one pointing into the sky. The trees, thick trunks spreading out strong branches, each green leaf held firm as it sprang out toward the sun, each, every, leaf entirely itself. Blind with seeing, Clothilde looked back to the water, where waves moved and the great tides swung underneath. Her hand spread out on the rock, and she looked at it, seeing its bones with the muscles spread over, and the skin encasing it. She lifted her hand and turned it over, moving her fingers slowly closed, and then open. The gray corrugated surface of the rock she sat on was dusted with gray-green lichen growing slowly outward to spread over the surface of the stone, and the gray stone itself almost grew outward from the earth, as if the earth sent forth stones into the light. Clothilde lifted her eyes in time to see the sleek brown body of a seal gather itself together and slip underwater, where silver fish swam, and hard-shelled clams backed down into the thick sandy mud, and the water rested heavy on the strong floor of the earth. Her skirt, she saw, was woven of hundreds of threads, each going on its own path over and under each other; and her hands touched the dark fabric that lay over her crossed legs. Clothilde stretched out on the rock, lying on her stomach, seeing.

When she woke up, she was not sure for a second where she was. The air had grown chilly and waves slapped up against the rocks. Clouds approached from the east. She stood up and looked at the woods. The trees had become only that again—they weren't each so crowdingly distinct.

Except, maybe—she peered into the woods with the wind blowing at her back and her skirt moving around her legs—the birches. She could see the swaying of the birches, and their delicate leaves scattered high along their branches, almost as she had seen them before she fell asleep, like the memory of a song.

Of course it hadn't happened. Clothilde knew that. It was a dream, or some temporary craziness that she should hope would never return.

But if, she thought, half believing, if it was true?

Then the peninsula wasn't hers, she remembered. The Voice had said no to that. So she didn't want it to be true. Not if the man in the boathouse could sell the peninsula now, so she wouldn't have it for when she needed it. Not if she couldn't go to college and be able to earn her own living so she could have her own life. Besides, it *was* hers, whatever the Voice said. It had been left to her in a will, and that was the law. Even if the law also said a father could take it away, the law said it was hers.

She'd have to just wait and see, Clothilde thought, running through the trees along her own path to the beach. She didn't believe it for a minute; but it would be something, if it were true. If she could have taken care of all those things. She wished she *had* asked to be prettier than Polly Dethier. It was all a dream, anyway, she decided. The nap had filled her with energy. It was all a dream, especially that strange way of seeing everything so clearly, the way everything had crowded itself into her eyes. Things were back to normal now. She'd rather have it be a dream, anyway, rather than craziness, if she could choose. If she could choose, she'd rather have it be true, she admitted, stumbling over a stone. But it couldn't be true. But if it were, time would tell. "Only time will tell," she laughed to herself.

If the things she asked for came about, she calculated, then she would know. And if they didn't? Well, it had been a wonderful dream, anyway. The nap and the dream had lifted her spirits. If that was all it was, she was still glad. There might be a way to keep the man in the boathouse from selling Speer Point, if she tried to think of it; she might be able to stop him, if she tried.

6

CLOTHILDE woke the very next morning, Monday, with sunrise in her heart, despite the fog that had come in overnight and wrapped itself around the house, crowding at her window. What if, Clothilde awoke thinking. What if it wasn't all a dream, what if—

She went into the bathroom, her mind full of possibilities. Her great-aunt hadn't pinched pennies on this farmhouse. Even for her tenants she had provided a thoroughly modern home. The bathroom was a big, tiled room, with a porcelain toilet and sink and tub, with deep shelves for storing towels. Clothilde wondered, scrubbing at her teeth and looking at the room reflected in the mirror, what the bathrooms in the cottage had been like, if this one in the farmhouse was so comfortable. Then she wondered what the cottage had looked like, and what it would have been like to live in it, if it hadn't burned down. And what if Father were to come walking out of the fog this morning, Father healed, handsome and lighthearted. What if he were to walk up through the swirling fog, and come home again; and she, Clothilde, would have made it happen. Clothilde smiled at her square face in the mirror, meeting her own eyes. Her eyes danced, like waves under sunlight.

She dressed quickly in her chilly bedroom, where wisps of fog brushed by the window. Downstairs, the kitchen was empty and cold. They didn't run the big coal furnace from late May to mid-September, to save money and to save the work, so the house was cold in the mornings, until the stoves were lit. Clothilde found her mother in the parlor, a shawl around her shoulders, sorting embroidery threads. Mother's fingers spread out the different colors onto the table beside her. The gas lamp gave out a warm light but that was the only warmth in the room; the wood stove sat in its corner like a cold black pumpkin.

Dierdre sat at Mother's feet, beside the deep bag in which Mother stored her fine needlework supplies. Clothilde hadn't seen that bag for four years. Mother hadn't had time for fancywork, in the last four years.

"I'm hungry," Dierdre greeted Clothilde.

"It's cold," Clothilde said. She took the fuel starter out of its container of kerosene and opened the door of the stove to lay the starter on the ashes. She built up a little pile of kindling on top of it, and added some medium-sized logs. When she stuck the long match in under the kindling, the kerosene-soaked starter caught fire immediately. Flames sprang up, as if they had just been waiting to be asked. Clothilde closed and latched the heavy metal door. She opened the vents wide, so the fire would burn hot, to warm up the heavy metal of the stove. Then she stood up to face her mother.

"I'm hungry," Dierdre insisted. "I want my breakfast."

Dierdre hadn't been given breakfast, the stove hadn't been lighted, and Mother was just sitting there sorting out colored threads.

"Do you feel all right?" Clothilde asked her mother.

"It's my hair," Mother answered. "I didn't have time to dress it properly," she said, as if that explained everything. "I'm a little hungry myself."

Mother's hair looked fine. She had it pulled back into a

thick knot at the back of her head. Big tortoise-shell pins held the twisted mass of hair in place. If Mother was hungry, and Dierdre was hungry, why hadn't she made anything to eat?

"Would you like me to make some oatmeal?" Clothilde offered.

"No," Dierdre said. "Pancakes."

"That would be fine, Clothilde," Mother answered. "I've often thought Lou shouldn't be allowed to sleep out Sunday nights. It's bad management to let servants do that. They don't get back in time for the morning meal." She turned her attention back to the threads. Clothilde went across to the cold kitchen.

Clothilde started a fire in the stove, opening the vents wide so it would burn hot. She put a pan of water on the stove, to heat. When it came to a boil, she added salt, butter, and a measure of oatmeal. The water foamed up and she stirred at the mass until it had reached the thick, slow boil at which the cereal would cook. Then she turned down the flame, covered the pan, and set bowls and spoons out on the table. From the cool cellar she brought up a pitcher of milk. From the cupboard she brought down the bowl of brown sugar.

It would be several minutes before the oatmeal had cooked, and Dierdre got cranky when she was kept waiting for her food, so Clothilde went back down to the cellar for an apple. She cut it into quarters and removed the core from each quarter before peeling off the skin. She set the four pieces in a bowl. She was wiping her hands on her apron as she went into the parlor. "I've got an apple for you, Dierdre," she said. "To keep the wolf away."

Dierdre jumped up, giggling at the wolf. Mother didn't even look up. One thing about Dierdre—if you gave her what she wanted she cheered up right away.

Clothilde kept an eye on her sister, to see that she didn't cram too much apple into her mouth at once, while she kept an eye on the oatmeal, where it bubbled away on the stove. When Dierdre climbed down from the table, Clothilde brushed her tangled hair, and braided it the way Mother liked. French braids had two small braids beginning at the top of your head; each smaller braid was then braided into the bigger pigtails. Clothilde couldn't do French braids for herself, but she could do it for Dierdre. "Pretty," she said, giving the little girl a hug.

"I'm pretty," Dierdre answered, satisfied.

"Pretty enough to go tell Mother that breakfast is ready?"

Dierdre considered this. "Yes," she decided.

Clothilde spooned oatmeal into bowls and sat down with Dierdre to wait for Mother. "Clothilde, dear, you mustn't sit down to table with your apron still on," Mother said. Clothilde obeyed without asking any questions, even though she would just have to put the apron back on again for the washing up. It was the fog that made Lou late, she thought.

Mother said the grace: "Bless this food to our use, and us to Thy service." They ate without talking. When Dierdre spilled cereal over the edge of her bowl, Mother ignored it, so it was left to Clothilde to warn her sister to eat carefully, and to mop up the spill. Clothilde finally asked her mother, "When did Nate leave?"

Mother looked at the clock. Clothilde also looked at the clock. It was well after eight. Lou was usually back by half-past seven. She wondered how thick the fog was, in the village.

"I think it was just after six," Mother said. "He wanted an early start, and with the fog . . . it's only a short sail across the bay to town, so he'll have arrived in good time. They wanted to catch the midday tide."

But the tide wasn't high at midday, and Nate knew that as well as Clothilde. By midday, the tide would be well out. Maybe Mother had misunderstood. She was paying so little attention to things that she might well have mistaken what Nate told her.

"Young men are so eager for things to happen," Mother said. She had only eaten half of her oatmeal, but she put her spoon down to show she was finished. "Always set out plates under bowls, dear," she reminded Clothilde, and then went back to the subject. "Nate was so excited. Young men like going off together, to have adventures." That made Clothilde think of all the young men going off to war. She thought Mother must be thinking the same thing, but her mother just looked gently amused, the way she did when Dierdre played house with Dolly Molly.

"Lou is really late," Clothilde said.

"You said you'd teach me to stitch," Dierdre told Mother.

"Servants are always as late as they can be. They're not reliable," Mother answered Clothilde. Then she turned to Dierdre. "Not this morning, dear. Mother's busy."

"But you said," Dierdre insisted.

"Don't talk back." Mother rose from the table. Dierdre tagged along behind her into the parlor.

Clothilde had finished washing their dishes and was drying out the saucepan when Lou came in. "I didn't hear you," Clothilde said. "You're late."

"Yuh, that fog muffles sound fine," Lou told her. "It'll burn off, mebbe." She sounded cheerful, as if she liked the fog.

Lou's good humor made Clothilde cross. "Did you get lost coming out? Is that why you're more than an hour late?"

"Oh no, I wouldn't get lost. Not on the road out here. I could walk that road blindfolded. No, we stayed up late, my ma and me, after we got back from services. We were jes' talking. So we slept in this morning, because my brother Jack kept the little ones fed and quiet. It was gone seven when I woke up."

"Talking about what?"

"Just—talk. He was out on one of his runs, see, so we had the big room to ourselves once the little children went asleep. With two to work, it doesn't take long at all to do, so we had time to sit together. And once we get started talking, we go on."

"What if he was arrested?" Clothilde asked. She didn't know why she did that, because it was almost as if she was trying to make Lou unhappy.

"Who's to catch him?"

"The revenue men."

"They don't know the water like our men do, they don't know the coast. The fog he'ps, too, yuh. That's not to say I'd be sorry if they did—except for the shame to my ma."

"But then how would you live?" Clothilde asked.

"My ma could work out some, if she didn't have him." Lou's mouth closed on the words and her face closed off. "If I'm working over away at one of the cottages, with higher wages. We could manage." Lou's good cheer had vanished.

Clothilde didn't want Lou to go somewhere else to work. She could imagine, too, how Lou would be treated in a house like her grandfather's. "You ought to just stay here," she muttered.

"If it was my choosing, I would. If it was your choosing, too, yuh. But it's never ours to choose, is it? Enough wool-gathering—it's washday. It'll be bad enough, the drying, with this fog, without putting off the washing. Will you help me with the water?"

Clothilde would. Lou's hands were clumsy with the heavy pots of steaming water, heated on the stove. This was the only chore that gave Lou any trouble, handling the big pots of water, filling them and setting them on the stove, then carrying them over to the washtub. As she ran water into the two big pots, Clothilde looked at her own hands. She could almost feel how Lou's hands must feel, her twisted fingers; for a minute she could—lifting up a full pot to carry it to the stove—see her own hand being caught into the machinery of the mill, being pulled in—she turned around to look at Lou, whose fingers were tying the apron around her waist. Lou's fingers were nimble enough. Clothilde guessed Lou was used to her hands.

While the water heated, Clothilde and Lou went upstairs and stripped the beds. While the linens soaked in soap and bluing, they remade the beds with fresh sheets, plumping up the pillows and pulling the bedcovers up straight and neat. Nate's bed didn't need fresh sheets.

Clothilde helped Lou scrub the linens against the corrugated washboard. It was a job she particularly hated, but the fog outside seemed to have seeped inside, and swirled with clammy confusion around her spirit, so that she took a bitter pleasure in the discomforts of hot water and heavy sheets, of the hard steel bruising her knuckles as she scrubbed. The weight of the sheets pulled at her shoulders. Her arms grew tired, achingly tired. The stove heated up the whole kitchen with the doors and windows closed against the fog; the whole room was steamy. Mother and Dierdre stayed in the parlor, playing with threads. The bitterness rolled around Clothilde like a fog, and she fed her own angers, like feeding logs into a fire to keep off the chill.

When she went outside to hang out the first of the sheets, Clothilde saw that Lou was right: the fog was lifting. Her circle of visibility extended about forty or fifty feet. Beyond that circle, the shadowy woods were blurred. After hanging out the sheets—and why even bother to do that Clothilde didn't know, on a day when they would become more damp every hour they hung there—Clothilde wandered over to look at the garden before going back inside. Laundry was Lou's chore, after all, not hers. She needn't feel guilty about taking a couple of minutes off. Her arms and shoulders were tired, her back was tired, and her fingers were cold and stiff—her heart was tired. Weeds had sprung up in the neglected garden, crowding the plants, so it was hard to see the neatly planted rows of vegetables. Mother should be out here weeding, Clothilde thought. Or Nate. Somebody should be taking care of the garden or they wouldn't have the vegetables to put up for winter. Even the Swiss chard was beginning to look choked off, and chard could grow through almost anything.

She dragged the laundry basket back inside.

Lou had wrung the towels damp, feeding them between the two wooden rollers and cranking at the handle. She piled them now into the basket.

Mother came to the door before Clothilde could get out of the room. Mother, in her green flowered dress, looked cool and fresh. "It's time for a cup of tea and Dierdre would like warmed milk," Mother said.

Lou's pale face looked up from the tub where she was scrubbing at the white blouses. She straightened up, nodding, drying her hands on her apron.

"And I need my hair done properly, Lou," Mother said. Lou looked quickly at Clothilde, and then away.

"Clothilde, I need Lou here, so I'm going to ask you to go to the store and see if Mrs. Grindle has a nice fowl."

"But it's Monday," Clothilde protested. Chicken on Monday? On Monday, they finished the chowder, if there was any left, along with Saturday's roast, if any remained.

"Your father always enjoyed creamed chicken over rice. Don't be slow with the tea, Lou," Mother said, turning to leave the room.

Clothilde wanted to run after her mother, before she had a chance to sit down again and pick up her fine needlework. She wanted to look right into Mother's face and say *Stop it,* say *Why aren't you working?* But you couldn't talk to your mother that way, that angry way. You couldn't quarrel with your mother. She was your mother.

Besides, Clothilde thought, she could leave right away for the village and not have to do any more laundry. She put down the basket and took off her apron. She rolled her sleeves down. She wasn't exactly pleased to be going to the village to pick out delicacies for the man in the boathouse, and she knew there was something wrong with Mother, but a walk sounded good to her. Even with the fog, a walk sounded good.

"Should I wrap up some bread and jam for you?" Lou asked.

"I'm not hungry, thanks," Clothilde answered. "And the garden needs weeding."

"She's been talking about flowers," Lou said. "She's been talking about rosebushes and dahlias, chrysanthemums and spring bulbs. I don't know where she'll get the money for flowers. I don't know what she'll do without me, yuh."

Clothilde took Nate's car jacket down from its hook by the door and went out, without even moving the laundry basket out of the way, without even bothering to answer Lou. Lou was right, so there wasn't anything to answer.

She walked along without thinking, just walking, following the driveway through fog-shrouded woods, up and down hills, until the land rose upward to form the narrow causeway that joined the peninsula to the mainland. There, no trees grew. There, the road was just wide enough for a single carriage, and the rocks fell away at either side of it. Mussels clung to the rocks down by the water, all sizes of mussels, from tiny half-inch babies up to big three-inch grandfathers. The mussel colonies made black stains on the sides of the rocks.

On the mainland, the fog lay much lighter. Hawkweed flowers shone yellow among the grass that sloped down to the water's edge. Hawkweed liked open expanses, Clothilde thought, watching the slow way the sun was burning away patches of fog. In the shady woods, it was white plumes of foamflower you saw, spreading along the floor of the woods as summer began. The foamflowers, which appeared and then disappeared as if summer were a tall lady walking through the woods with a lacy train to her dress, could only grow in the cool shadowy woods, where trees and broad-leafed ground cover gave them a sense of protection. The wood lily, however, liked only those in-between places, where woods turned into meadows; there and nowhere else they bloomed out, reaching up to the sky with their bright orangy-red hands cupped to catch the sunlight. Every flower had its season and its own particular place, Clothilde thought. She walked along at an easy pace. She was in no hurry to reach her destination, no hurry to return once her errand was done. If she could have spent the whole day on the quiet road, she'd not have minded.

Her eyes lingered over the golden hawkweed, and suddenly her mouth gasped for air.

How could she have forgotten? How could something like the Voice have happened—or even just maybe happened, maybe not been a dream—and she forget it for a single minute? If it was true—

She peered at the field that she was slowly walking past, grasses and flowers. It remained a field of grass and flowers, nothing like the overwhelming vision of each shape and hue that she had seen—or thought she had seen, maybe she had dreamed it—yesterday afternoon. She wished she could still see things that way, but she was already forgetting what that way was, she could see that. Like a dream fading from memory.

Clothilde jammed her hands into the pockets of Nate's jacket, and stepped out briskly. There were only two possibilities. Either it was real and true, or she was losing her mind. She had asked for three—no, four—things. If those things were to come to pass, then she would know. And if they didn't come to pass?

It made her sad, knowing how much she could not see, looking around her. She was like a blind person who'd been given sight for about two minutes, then had to go back to blindness.

If these things never came to pass, if Nate went ahead on his cruise, and Lou's father kept on in his bad ways, if the man in the boathouse weren't made better, healed, and—

She remembered then that when she had asked that Speer Point be hers, the answer had been No. So if it stayed hers, that would be a backward answer.

What if these things never happened? Then she could keep on waiting, or she could admit that there was something wrong with her. But no matter what was true, there was nothing she could do right then except wait and see.

7

CLOTHILDE followed the road on into the village, going through the woods first, and then past the outlying farms. The Henderson farm was farthest out from town. It was their many children that enabled Mr. Henderson to also work the fields on Speer Point. He grew feed crops out there, because they needed less care and that left his own acres for market crops and grazing pastures. A foggy haze hung over the Hendersons' big farmhouse, the barns, and the surrounding fields. A couple of the Hendersons' sons were walking from the barn to the house; a few cows grazed on a hillside, four-legged shapes in the fog.

Clothilde walked steadily along the hilly road, not hurrying, not dawdling. The smell of the ocean was in the air, although woods and slopes hid the water from view. The last farm outside of the village belonged to the Twoheys. Their house was at the crossroads where the rough farm tracks joined the more traveled road where you turned left into the village, or right, off to the northwest and the larger towns. At the Twoheys' the curtains were drawn and the three cows that the farm's few acres could support stood in the mud of the fenced barnyard. The house gave a blank, silent face to the road.

Clothilde followed the flat dirt road to the left, passing the one-room, one-story schoolhouse. Over the summer weeks, grass grew up wild around the little shingled building. Queen Anne's lace had rushed into the schoolyard during June and now looked like a veil the fog had spread out to dry over the top of the long grasses. Butter-and-eggs, like drops of sunlight that had been left behind, crowded up beside the shingled walls.

When they had first come to Maine, Mother had planned to plant flowers, planned to surround their house with beds of tulips and daffodils, dahlias and chrysanthemums, planned a rose garden. But there was no time for flowers, as it turned out, and Clothilde was just as glad. The stiff formal gardens at Grandfather's house gave her no pleasure. Neither did the neatly planted beds in the yards of the houses near her school in Manfield, with their bright-faced flowers looking as if they wanted to escape from behind the white picket fences. Clothilde didn't like planted gardens; she liked the accidental flowers of woods and fields, and the way they came unexpectedly into bloom, into sight.

She descended into the village, two stores and a dozen houses spread irregularly out over hillsides that dropped down to the harbor. That foggy day, the water lay still and the square shapes of the boats hung motionless on it, like half-formed ideas. Sturdy masts rose up into the misty air. Fog was more dangerous than winds or waves, so nobody went out on a foggy day if he could help it. A man who knew the coastal waters could bring his boat safely to harbor during a storm, or could keep it out in deep water, away from the dangers of the shore. But in fog, a man could get confused and lose his bearings entirely, and be on the rocks before he knew he was anywhere near them; or he might sail out into the thick air and never be seen again.

Even over the harbor the fog was already half mist, with just the occasional thick cloud blown down it from open water. It probably wasn't a fog that would lie over the land for days. It wasn't even that thick: a thick fog devoured color, turning everything gray or black. Clothilde could see the yellow light inside Grindle's general store, and the dark red of the blacksmith's barn. She could see, now that the dock was visible, the greens and browns and blacks of the dresses of the women gathered there. The women all faced the same direction, as if they were answering the slow summoning call of the foghorn. As she looked down on it, the group broke apart and came up the hill, singly or in pairs. Mrs. Grindle was among the women, as was Polly Dethier. Mrs. Grindle wore the white jacket that she put on when she worked behind the counter. Polly wore a bright white pinafore over her yellow dress. Clothilde didn't stay to watch them come up the steep roadway from the dock, she didn't stay to talk. She went into Grindle's store.

Mr. Grindle was behind the counter. When he saw who she was, he leaned toward her, his round eyes bulging with curiosity. He asked how the family was, out on the Point, and Clothilde said they were all well. He asked if they didn't mind the isolation, and she said No, they didn't. He asked if they weren't bothered by strangers out there, and Clothilde, knowing now what the secrets were his eyes were wondering about, said No, they weren't bothered by strangers. That was true, too. Mr. Grindle gave up, then, and asked her what he could do for her. She asked him for a fowl, ready for the pot. He fetched one out from the back room where an icebox kept meat and poultry fresh. He held the pale plucked chicken by its limp neck, waiting for her approval. Clothilde nodded, so he went to the marble counter and cut off the head and feet with a cleaver.

He didn't talk with her while he did that, as if his thoughts were miles away. He wrapped the bird in stiff butcher's paper, and tied it around. Then he handed it to her.

"But you haven't weighed it," Clothilde reminded him. "You haven't marked it down in your book."

"Oh yes," he said, taking it back from her. "There's a boat out," he said, to explain his oversight.

"Not in this weather." Clothilde had lived here long enough to know why he was worried. "He'll wait out the fog," she suggested. "Was he out before it came in this morning?"

Mr. Grindle shook his head. "He was expected back at dawn. He should have been back by first light. The fog came in around midnight, Paul Dethier says." Mr. Grindle's eyes focused on her then. "Paul was up with his bad stomach."

As Mr. Grindle wrote Clothilde's purchase into his book, his wife returned. At the sound of the ringing bell, Mr. Grindle and Clothilde both looked around. Mrs. Grindle pursed her thin lips and shook her head.

"Lou told me, Mr. Small was out away last night," Clothilde said.

"It's my sister's husband's boat," Mrs. Grindle answered, as if she were scolding Clothilde. She was a scolding kind of woman anyway, so Clothilde didn't pay much attention to her tone. "As if my sister didn't have enough worry to keep her awake nights, there's Joseph Twohey has to go running those risks. And in that man's company. And now look what's come to them—going out on a Sabbath evening, for that purpose. There's been a judgment on him, that's for sure."

"That's a harsh thought, Mrs. Grindle," Mr. Grindle said. "With the child listening to you, and all."

"It's the Lord's truth I'm speaking, and it's no more than you're thinking yourself," Mrs. Grindle answered, but she closed her mouth over the subject.

Clothilde guessed that everybody in town must know about the smuggling of whiskey, but nobody talked about it. When she thought of Jeb Twohey, who would never now be able to give his family the help on the farm or boat that children should, she thought she understood why people didn't talk. "Fog's lifting," was all she could think of. She picked up the wrapped chicken.

"Don't you count on it," Mrs. Grindle answered, her lips pursed.

Mr. Grindle wished Clothilde a good day and she left the store, her exit marked by the ringing of the bell hung over the door.

Outside, the sky had closed in again, covering the village with fine moisture. Clothilde looked down the hill toward the long harbor, where steep hillsides framed the still water. From its mouth, a cloud of fog swirled toward her. She hurried down the steep path to meet it.

Out on the end of the long wooden dock, high above the lowering water, she waited for the fog to reach her. Fingers of fog blew toward her, white tendrils reaching out. The air on her face was cold, moist. The cloud rolled toward her, hiding everything in its path, until it wrapped itself around her. She could see nothing there, nothing but thick streaks of fog moving, encircling her. She was alone there in the fog, alone in the world. The foghorn wound its mournful note around her. Clothilde knew better than to try to walk back to land; she stood still, savoring the mysteriousness and the safe danger. Sense of direction was one of the first things you lost, in such a fog. She might easily, thinking she was going back along the dock to the land, step off it and fall the fifteen feet to the water below. If she were not unconscious after the fall, she might call out for help—but in fog, voices were almost impossible to locate.

Clothilde shivered, at the thought, at the chill in the air; but it was a pleasurable fear. As long as she didn't move, she was safe.

As the cloud moved on by, carried along on the breeze, the mist around her lightened and she could almost see the shapes of the hillsides that enclosed the harbor. Then, with only a few thin, reluctant fingers wisping back at her, the fog was gone. Clothilde turned around and saw two figures, standing together at the start of the dock, beside a pile of lobster traps. It was as if the figures had come out of nowhere, as if they had just materialized there. The two figures stepped forward, hands clasped, one tall, broad shouldered, the other short and pulling forward. It was Jeb Twohey, and his mother.

Mrs. Twohey didn't look much like her sister, except for the pursed expression of her mouth. Her thin neck rose out of the coat's dark collar and she barely noticed Clothilde, except to nod her head.

"Good morning," Clothilde answered. She shouldn't have said that, she knew right away. She didn't know what you said to a woman whose husband's boat was hours late coming in, with a fog at sea. Jeb held onto his mother's hand like a four-year-old who was afraid of getting lost and being talked to by strangers. The high-necked sweater he wore looked too large for him, and his damp hair lay flat on his head. "Hello, Jeb," Clothilde said. She'd never spoken to him before. Mrs. Twohey didn't let people get close enough to Jeb to say anything. Clothilde didn't know what to say to Jeb, either, and she doubted that he even knew who she was. There was nothing strange in that, since he had been gone to war by the time her family arrived at Speer Point, and he'd been kept hidden away since his return to the village.

Jeb nodded his head, looking back at her over his shoulder, again, like a four-year-old being kept close by his mother. His eyes went to the package she was holding. "It's a chicken," Clothilde told him, even though he hadn't asked. She thought he was wondering what it was, so she told him.

"It's dead," he told her.

Clothilde stared into his eyes. She didn't know what to say, it was so strange to hear that deep man's voice coming from that face. Jeb's face, with its thick nose and broad jaw, didn't seem alive at all, except for the eyes, which were staring and staring at the package Clothilde held. Jeb's face looked empty, as if there were nothing inside it. Finally, Clothilde said, agreeing with him, "Yes."

Mrs. Twohey, holding tight to Jeb's big hand, ignored them. She was peering into the white mists at the mouth of the harbor.

"Yes, it's dead," Clothilde repeated.

Jeb looked at Clothilde's face then, his eyes meeting hers, as if he had expected her to say something else, to deny that the chicken was dead. But why would she do that? she wondered.

"It's less work to prepare if the butcher does the slaughtering. Less work for my mother," she explained, as if he were a little child.

Jeb Twohey's eyes stayed staring into hers and she had to look back at him. She saw tears gathering there, and spilling out. The foghorn sounded, and he cringed back against his mother with his eyes still on Clothilde.

It was crazy behavior, no question; but if what she had seen in her dream had been anything like the truth, Clothilde could understand his misery. For all that he was so big and broad, Jeb Twohey should never have had to go to war. She knew, as if she could see right into the black swirling fog of his brain, that nothing could ever make him right again.

Clothilde wanted to get away, but she didn't know how to. She ought, she thought, to say something, but she didn't know if you were supposed to mention what people were really worrying about. There were so many things you weren't supposed to say outright, but she didn't know what else to talk about and until she had made at least one comment, she couldn't leave.

"I think maybe the fog is lifting," she finally said. She said it to Jeb because Mrs. Twohey's narrow back was facing her. Mrs. Twohey made a small humphing noise that might have been a response, but Jeb answered her. "The things that grow upward like the sunlight. The things that grow downward like the rain."

"Hush you now," Mrs. Twohey said, turning around to look at him and then turning back to look out to the harbor's mouth, as if she were too tired even to scold.

"But it's true," Jeb said. His masklike face gave Clothilde no clue about what to answer. "Things grow so quietly," he explained.

"Yes, that's true," Clothilde agreed. "I have to go home now. Good-bye, Jeb. Good-bye, Mrs. Twohey." She hurried away. When she looked back from the end of the dock, Jeb was still watching her. She raised a hand but, although she knew he saw her, he didn't raise his hand in answer.

Poor Jeb Twohey, Clothilde thought. But it was more than a thought. It was a force of feeling pushed up through her like the force that drove rocks up through the surface of the land. She had seen Jeb before, with his blank face and his awkward way of walking, but she had never spoken with him, or looked at his eyes, so she had not known what queer, simple words he used. Before she hadn't tried to hear the disjointed ideas that floated around inside his head, floating around in that thick black fog. She was so lost in thought that she almost ran head-on into the men who were coming down the hillside. "Steady now," a voice said, and she looked up to see Tom Hatch among four others.

"I'm sorry." Clothilde stepped aside to let them pass. The others went on, talking about the lifting fog, but Tom Hatch stayed with Clothilde. He was a small man, thin and wiry, but he gave the impression of being larger than he was. He had thick curly dark hair and quick brown eyes.

"We might be able to take a boat out," he told her, as if she had asked him what he was doing. "To make a search," he added. "If it'd been me, out last night, I'd have headed for a harbor, if I could, when I saw the fog. I'd have anchored, to wait it out. Or I might have headed out away, into open water."

"Then what good will a search be?" Clothilde asked. She didn't know why he had stopped to tell her this.

"Because there's other things could happen, and they might not have had either of those choices. So it might be, some kind of help is needed. If the fog's in truth lifting."

"I can't tell if it is or not," Clothilde told him. The heavy sweater he wore would keep out both damp and cold, so she suspected that Tom Hatch wasn't sure either. Something made her ask: "Why weren't you in the war, Mr. Hatch?" He had been available to help them when they first moved to Speer Point, helping them make the skiff seaworthy and teaching Nate how to use it. She had occasionally seen him in the village, but he'd never been in uniform.

"Yuh, but I was. In the Coast Guard—they needed men who know the coast."

"Oh," Clothilde said.

"It kept me near to home, some of the time, when we weren't hunting submarines. My brother went to France."

"Oh," Clothilde said.

"He didn't come back."

"I'm sorry," Clothilde said.

"Yuh. I was the lucky one, whether I deserve it or not."

"I guess that's why you're going out now," Clothilde said. She didn't know where that idea had come from. The voices of the men called up from the dock, calling him down to join them.

"Mebbe so," Tom Hatch answered.

"I wish you luck," Clothilde answered.

"So you might tell Lou, if she's fretting, that we'll do whatever we can, miss."

He was running down the hillside before she could answer. Clutching at her package, Clothilde went back up to the village street.

8

Wₕₑₙ she reached the top of the hill, Clothilde could see the whole of the village, the Grindles' store with its wooden porch and post office flag hanging limp, the big square farming supplies business the Dethiers owned, the blacksmith's barn, and the shingled church across the street flanked on one side by the minister's house and on the other by the cemetery.

Clothilde turned to look down at the dock. It looked like the men were going to go out in Tom Hatch's boat; the figures on the dock were climbing down the long wooden ladder into a dinghy. She put the wrapped chicken down and took off Nate's coat. The air was growing warmer. Her arms full of coat and chicken, she turned to go home.

"Clothilde? Clothilde, wait."

Polly Dethier was hurrying down the street toward her. What would Polly Dethier want with her? In that flowered yellow dress with the ruffles on her pinafore starched stiff, and her hair in long curls that shone like hawkweed.

Polly had eyes the color of Michaelmas daisies and a little pink mouth. She was fourteen and she had a figure. "Hello," she said. "It's been a long time since I've seen you." When Polly smiled, a dimple appeared in her cheek.

Her skin wasn't browned by the sun, but dusted with the sun's color, creamy gold. "Hasn't it?" she asked.

Clothilde didn't say anything. She felt plain and brown and like a little girl. She didn't have anything to say, and Polly hadn't asked her a question anyway, nothing that needed an answer. Clothilde held the wrapped chicken close to her chest and looked at Polly's pretty face.

"How are you?" Polly asked. "Do you miss school?"

"No." Clothilde shook her head.

"How's your family?" Polly asked.

"Fine."

"I guess," Polly said, holding Clothilde there by talking to her, "they're going out to look for Mr. Twohey. Did you hear about that?"

Clothilde nodded. She shifted her feet. She didn't have anything to say to Polly and Polly didn't have anything to say to her. They were the closest to each other in age at school, but they weren't friends.

Clothilde thought Polly would go on about her business then. She didn't know what Polly wanted, and neither, apparently, did Polly, who just stood there for a while before she finally said, "Isn't summer boring? Except for socials and Independence Day, what is there to do but sit in the shade."

"We have plenty to do," Clothilde said. She couldn't imagine Polly Dethier's life away from school. She didn't want to ask any questions, but she was a little curious about what it would be like to be Polly. If she was going to have to stand here talking with the girl, she might as well satisfy her curiosity. "What do you do?"

"Oh, it's dull. My mother has all these notions about how I'm supposed to—I have to practice piano, and I go up to town to take drawing lessons, I have needlework—sitting up straight and listening to them talk. Do you want to hear something? Sometimes," Polly confided, smiling and leaning her head closer to Clothilde, "I would rather be a boy."

Clothilde didn't much believe that.

"They can go swimming and fishing, even camp out. They have things to do. Doesn't your brother have lots to do during vacations?"

Polly wasn't saying exactly what she wanted to say, Clothilde thought, but she didn't know what it was Polly really wanted to know. "I guess," she answered.

"Oh, I do admire your family," Polly said, her cheeks pink. "The way you carry on, even though Mr. Speer was so tragically killed, and your whole life changed so much, and all."

Clothilde just stared at the girl. That was what the village thought, then, that Mother was a war widow. But Lou hadn't said anything to her about that, so where had Polly gotten that idea? She shifted from one foot to the other, not wanting to lie, not wanting to tell the truth.

"I'm sorry, Clothilde," Polly apologized. "I shouldn't have brought that up. Mother says I haven't ever learned to control my tongue."

Clothilde didn't know what to say to that, either.

"Do you think the fog will be lifted, out at sea?" Polly asked.

"I don't know," Clothilde answered: How could she know what the weather was like off shore?

"Anyway," Polly said, "we're going to have a new teacher in the fall. Father went into Bangor last week, to interview candidates."

"What happened to Mrs. Barstow? She didn't say anything about not teaching us next year."

"Mrs. Barstow's sister's family is going to move out to Seattle, Washington. Her brother-in-law will have a better job. She decided to go with them." Polly always knew all about the teachers, because her father was the first selectman of the village, and so he did the hiring as well as boarding them in his big house. "I think Mrs. Barstow hopes to find another husband," Polly added, and giggled.

Clothilde hated that giggle. "What's wrong with that?"

Polly didn't even notice her ill humor. "My father says that there's no danger this new teacher, Miss Winkle, will do that. He says she's as plain as a pikestaff and well over thirty."

Clothilde planned, starting right then, to like Miss Winkle.

"I only have two more years so it won't bother me what she's like, and then—can you keep a secret?"

Clothilde nodded, although she didn't think Polly had any secrets worth keeping.

"Because I might have a coming out party. I'm maybe going to be a debutante. Mother wants me to. Isn't that—nobody in the village has ever had a coming out party. If Mother gets her way—it's Father who's objecting—it'll be at my uncle's house, in Bangor, and we'll invite everybody. Just everybody. And it'll be a dance, too. You have to wear a long white dress, and your hair up, and have two escorts too, and—I could ask you, even though you'll be a little young, exceptions are made. Because your family is . . . you know. Won't that be fun?"

Clothilde was spared thinking up an answer by the sound of a motorcar. In the quiet air, you could hear the putt-putting of the motor before the vehicle crested the hill. The car was coming down the road that led away to the northwest, from one of the summer cottages over to town, probably. By the time it entered the village, the Grindles had stepped out onto their porch and Mr. Dethier stood at the door of his store, watching.

It looked as if the automobile was going to rush right through the village, but it made a hasty halt just a few feet beyond where the two girls stood. The two figures riding in the high front seat pushed up their goggles and took off their hats, before climbing out. The motor putt-putted, one of the noisy gasoline-powered engines. The red metal body gleamed with wax and the silver spokes shone with polishing. The driver stood beside the engine, listening, then reached inside the vehicle to stop the motor. Then they turned around.

They were young to be driving, Clothilde thought. They looked alike, although one was a stocky redhead with freckles and the other a slender dark-haired young man. They looked alike because they both looked as if they were glad to be themselves, and as if they were about to laugh out loud. They looked alike because under the short car jackets, they both wore bright white trousers with crisp pleats and shoes that were as brightly polished as the automobile.

"The one person we wanted to see," the red-haired driver greeted Polly. He didn't even see Clothilde. "Alex? Fetch the charts out, will you? No, honestly, Polly, I said so to Alex, before we even pushed the starter button. He'll testify, won't you, Alex? I said to him that if we didn't find Polly Dethier at home, the whole trip would be wasted. Didn't I, Alex?"

"Or words to that effect."

"Alex, you are as stuffy as your grandfather," the redhead laughed. "Words to that effect," he mimicked his friend's voice. "It must be all that old money, you were born with your shirt already stuffed. Whatever he says, Polly, it's true that the only reason I came was to see you."

"You—you're teasing," Polly said. She stood quietly, looking down at the ground the way a young lady should. It was Clothilde who was staring.

"It had nothing whatsoever to do with a chance to take the Olds out for a spin," the dark-haired boy explained.

Polly was smiling at the ground, and her dimple showed. Clothilde decided to leave, but Polly reached out and held her elbow, holding her there.

"That's right," the redhead laughed. "You're the only reason, Polly."

"You're trying to make me vain," Polly answered.

"Pretty girls ought to be vain," he said, and she shook

her head at him, and went *ttch* as if she were scolding him. "Nate went off," he said, "and left his boat at our dock, with orders for us to return it. We need someone to show us exactly where, on this uninhabitable coast, we should take it. He also gave us a message to deliver."

Polly raised her head at that, and Clothilde saw an expression in her blue eyes that she couldn't name, something bright and happy, with nothing kept hidden. "Is it that I have to read the charts for you in order to hear my message?" Polly asked. Eager—happy and eager, that's what her eyes were.

"Now that would be ungentlemanly of us. Practically blackmail."

"Are you setting up as a gentleman now?" Polly asked. "My, my, I am impressed."

"She's got you properly pegged, Bobby," Alex said, coming back from the car with a nautical chart, which he spread out on the ground. Clothilde looked at it: it was a chart of the bay, she saw; she recognized Speer Point's mitten shape. *Mine*, she thought, with a smile she didn't let show, as she looked down at the chart.

"Inscrutable, isn't it?" the dark-haired boy said, looking at her.

"No," Clothilde answered.

He laughed at that, as if she had meant to be funny. "Who is this gracious young person?" he asked Polly. "Aren't you going to introduce us?"

"This is Nate's sister, Clothilde. Clothilde—meet Alex and Bobby."

"You're some of Nate's friends?" Clothilde had never met any of her brother's school friends. She felt differently about them, if they were friends of Nate's.

"We're more than that, Miss Speer. We are his great friends," Alex said, bowing his head at her.

"You see before you two of the Three Musketeers," Bobby added.

"One for all, and all for one," Alex added.

"Waiting only for D'Artagnan," Bobby added.

Clothilde didn't know what they were talking about but she knew what they meant. "David and Jonathan," she said, to show them that she could show off too.

Alex looked at her; he hadn't looked at her before. "One hopes it won't come to that," he said. "You are as sharp as a tack, aren't you?"

Sharper, Clothilde said to herself, but she didn't say it out loud. Neither did she stick out her tongue at him, even though she was tempted. She just looked right back at him.

"What are you talking about?" Polly demanded, claiming their attention. "Bobby, what are they talking about?"

"Your guess is as good as mine," Bobby laughed. Being sharp as a tack wasn't what they thought she ought to be, Clothilde thought; and she didn't give two hoots for what they thought.

"What we need," Alex said, "is someone to show us on the chart where we take Nate's boat. He gave us strict orders, didn't he, Bobby?"

"He did indeed. It was most unlike him. He was quite severe with us. We shall not, for one, take it around the Point to the boathouse, where we might be seen from the cottage. The beautiful reclusive mama, you know, shut away in her grief. I don't mean to be flippant," he apologized to Clothilde. "I mean, I think it's pretty wonderful all that loyalty to the dead hero. I do, it's just the way I always talk."

Clothilde didn't know what to say. Polly didn't say anything either.

"So we're supposed to leave it off in the cove on the north side. There's a mooring," Alex explained to Polly.

"But we shall not, for the second point, make ourselves known to the tenant farmer's family," Bobby said. "As if I needed warning about that. The natives—with certain most attractive exceptions—are as foreign as aborigines to me.

According to Nate, if we could execute this maneuver in the dead of night, under cover of dense fog, that would suit everyone best. It's like some spy drama, isn't it?" His laugh invited them to join in.

"So, if you'd show us where we'll find the mooring?" Alex asked Clothilde.

She hunkered down beside the chart and put her finger on the cove by the beach. Alex took a gold pencil out of his pocket to mark the place. "How about rocks, and tides?"

"Except for dead low tide there's enough water in the cove," she told him, without looking up from the chart. On a chart the mittened hand held onto its place by digging its claws into the water. "If you stay away from shore there's nothing to worry about."

"That's fine then. Thanks," he said. She got up, and picked up the wrapped chicken. He studied the chart. "It is a nice bit of property, Speer Point. I've never noticed how large it is."

Bobby stepped over to look down at the chart. "My father says it's worth a pretty penny already. When the old lady bought it, it was too far away for most people. Nobody would have guessed then how its value would rise, with the automobile making everything easier to get to. You could put half a dozen large estates on it, couldn't you?"

"Your father is a lunatic about land development," Alex said, folding the chart and getting up.

"He knows how to make money," Bobby agreed. "He actually—and he was at least half serious—made Nate an offer for it at one point. But Nate's too smart to sell now. He told Father he was planning to hold onto the Point and let its value continue to rise."

"Nate said that?" Clothilde asked, too amazed to keep her mouth shut.

"Now that it's his, now that your father—" Bobby started to say, then let the words drift away. "I'm sorry, I shouldn't sound so callous, and him a hero, too. It sounds like I don't have any patriotic feelings."

"I've got to go," Clothilde said, into the center of the group, not looking at any of them.

"May we give you a ride?" Alex offered. "It's not one of your Speer Electrics, but you might find the added power exhilarating."

"No," Clothilde said. "I'd rather walk."

"Whatever you prefer," Bobby said, not even waiting before he said to Polly, "And about the message we were entrusted with, to deliver it to you."

"A message?" Polly asked. Polly's voice sounded as if she'd forgotten the message, but her eyes lit up again.

Clothilde turned and walked away, but she listened to the voices behind her. "Nate says, we're to take you back into town with us, and buy you a soda. Or a sundae if you'd prefer that."

"Oh he does, does he?" Polly's voice had hesitated before it answered.

"With the permission of your formidable mother, of course," Bobby said.

Clothilde walked out of earshot, down through the village and up the hill beyond. It wasn't until she had passed the Twoheys' farm that she let herself start thinking.

The lies Nate had been telling—all those lies, and why had he been telling them? The friends he'd been making, if those were his friends.

Fog swirled in around her again. The temperature fell, but she didn't notice it, walking hard. Those two boys, and Nate too, she could see the world they lived in, sunlit and easy, an amusing place. Not like Jeb Twohey's world, the land that lay behind his blank face and dazed eyes. And Polly—Polly loved Nate. Clothilde suddenly knew that. And she knew that that was what Nate wanted Polly to do, or that was what Polly thought he wanted. The expression in Polly's eyes, that bright painful expression, was hope.

Clothilde didn't know why she was suddenly seeing into peoples' heads like this. She wished she wouldn't. She liked it better when she didn't think she knew what people thought or wanted, or were afraid of or were hoping for. When she had crossed the causeway to stand on her own land again, she stopped for a minute, to let her spirit ease. *Mine,* she thought, with the shrouded birches beside her and the rocks falling away into the invisible water. *Mine,* the dirt road underfoot. It was there under her feet, deep and steady, the whole peninsula.

Nate was truly gone, then, off on his cruise. She worked it out as she followed the road back home. Since Nate was off, it had in fact been a dream. It had been the strangest dream she'd ever had, and probably would ever have, but she could guess why she had had it: hoping that something would stop what was happening. But Nate was gone, off cruising, and the man in the boathouse wouldn't get better. He'd always have that face as long as he lived. Lou wouldn't find any way to get away from her father, either. She'd be stuck with having him hurt her, and having to give her family the money she earned because her father spent his lawless earnings on whiskey for himself, and nobody could stop him.

On the other hand, Clothilde thought, that might mean that the peninsula was going to stay hers after all. The Yeses in her dream turned into Noes, so the No had to turn into a Yes. Maybe. Because it *was* hers, she could feel it being hers, with every step she took on it, in the woods or on the beach, and on the headlands especially.

9

T HAT evening, Clothilde sat in the parlor unstitching the cloak. What a long day it had been, she thought, although she couldn't think why the day had seemed so long. Yesterday seemed a hundred years gone. The minutes of this Monday had lined up like the hundreds and thousands of tiny stitches along the seams of the cloak. There were so many stitches she couldn't count the ones behind her, or ahead of her, as if there were no end and no beginning to them. That was the way this day felt to her.

That thought didn't make her unhappy. In fact, Clothilde was feeling content. The red parlor curtains were pulled closed against the weather. Warmth spread out from the pot-bellied stove. Deep reds and blues were braided in concentric circles to make the rag rug. The lamplight fell warm on her hands. Lou had put Dierdre to bed and was finishing up the kitchen. Clothilde picked out stitch after stitch. Now the cloak would be a farewell gift for Lou. The wool, cleverly cut, would make a warm dress, the lining would make two good blouses. As her hands worked, separating the long seams, she reminded herself that two fine pieces of cloth were better than nothing, as a gift. Across from her, Mother's head was bent over a square of silk, onto which she was embroidering red and yellow flowers. The threads gleamed in the lamplight, and Mother's hair shone.

They were a houseful of women now. There was something peaceful about that idea. Boys, men, were forever going out and doing things, disturbing the quiet with the demands of their important businesses. Girls, women, stayed home, performing their small tasks. Even if the whole world crumbled around them, or fell away from beneath them, they worked patiently away. On a night like this, Clothilde thought, she didn't envy Nate his cruise, the new places, the adventure. A slow, foggy rain fell through the darkness outside. She was glad not to be out in this night.

Oddly, she remembered that strange dream. Really, it was a wonderful dream to have had, especially the way of seeing things that happened at the end of her dream. Such colors and such shapes—each leaf on every branch of all the trees. It was like being in a magic land, where everything was more perfectly itself. She smiled to herself. She kept forgetting it and then for some reason remembering. Maybe she remembered now because she was sitting quiet, like some wild animal in its den, like a rabbit snug in its hole. She wondered if it was possible to see people in that magical way—and then thought of Jeb Twohey, and the black fog that swirled around inside his head, and how it was as if he himself were huddled in there, like a rabbit waiting in the darkness of its burrow. It was Jeb Twohey who needed dreams like the one she'd had. She could just imagine what his dreams were like, poor soul. Her dream, now—and it wasn't just trees, it was the rocks too, it was everything she had looked at; remembering, Clothilde smiled.

"It's lovely, isn't it?" Mother asked.

Recalled from her own thoughts, Clothilde didn't understand at first what her mother was asking. Instead of looking at the needlework Mother had spread out over her lap, she looked at her mother, at the oval face under a dark cloud of hair, at eyes the blue of a summer sky, which shone there like the sunlit sky. Mother was prettier even than Polly Dethier—by far. Mother was waiting, holding up the work now for Clothilde's approval. In her eyes, Clothilde saw how much Mother wanted Clothilde to approve. "What?" Clothilde asked.

"It wasn't anything." Mother lay the piece down, her eyes clouded.

"It is lovely," Clothilde finally understood. "It's very pretty. I don't see how you get such fine stitches," she said, knowing that was what Mother wanted to hear.

"I had good teachers," Mother explained, cheered. Her hands smoothed the fabric. Her fingers traced the stitched flowers. "I always liked pretty things. And flowers, too. The shop where I worked sold flowers."

"You worked in a shop? You worked in a flower shop? You never told me."

"It was before I married, so—everything changed when I married."

"Why did you work in a shop?" Clothilde hadn't known Mother could surprise her.

"We had to support ourselves," Mother said. "The orphanage couldn't take care of us all our lives. The woman who owned the shop—Mrs. Peters, Mrs. Mary Peters—she was a widow and a good churchgoer. She liked orphanage girls. I was fortunate to have that employment offered to me. She had no children of her own. She gave me my own room, in her apartment over the shop, and I'd never had my own room before."

Clothilde couldn't imagine it. She had never thought about her mother's life. She had a hundred questions she wanted to ask. She wondered what wages Mother had earned and what it had been like to work behind the counter, serving customers. She wondered what kinds of customers there had been, and if it had been in a city, a city store. She had never thought her mother could be a shopgirl. "What kind of work did you do?" she asked.

Mother shook her head. She didn't want to answer. Why didn't she want to answer? Before Clothilde could ask again, there was a knock at the door.

The sound seemed to boom through the quiet house. Clothilde stared at her mother: She couldn't think of who it might be, unless it might be the man from the boathouse. She didn't want to answer the door. But Mother wasn't getting up either. They never had visitors at night, or during the day either. The knocking at the door—which was repeated now, more loudly—sent the quiet flying out of the house.

"Louisa?" Mother called. "Answer the door."

Clothilde wanted to protest, to say Lou was busy and she could see who was there, but she didn't know who it could be and she didn't want to be the first to find out. From her chair, she watched Lou hurry to the door and step back, opening it.

A man stood there, dressed in yellow oilskins. He took off his jacket and shook the water off it before he would step into the hallway. It was Tom Hatch.

Tom Hatch stood inside the door with his jacket in his hand. He wore high black rubber boots and the waterproof trousers were held up by wide suspenders. "Is Mrs. Speer in?" he asked Lou.

"Yuh, they're in the parlor."

"It's Tom Hatch," Clothilde told her mother. Her mother's large eyes looked even larger; she too was surprised and anxious at this visit.

Her voice, however, sounded calm. "Come in, Mr. Hatch."

He came no farther than the door, so he wouldn't drip onto the rug. What news had brought him out, Clothilde wondered. She didn't think she wanted to hear it, but she wished he would hurry and speak, to get it over with. Tom Hatch wore a heavy sweater and he was fumbling in the trouser pockets, under his oilskin pants.

"It's a bad night to be out in," Mother said.

"It'll do," Tom Hatch answered. "I'm here because—this came for you." He reached over to hand Mother a yellow envelope, a telegram. "Mr. Grindle didn't know but what you should have it right away. They sent it over from the Western Union office in town, but the delivery boy didn't want to risk the road out here, in this weather and at night."

Mother held the envelope in her hand. "I thank you for your trouble."

"It was no trouble. When a man has no family, it's no trouble for him to go out of an evening. Besides, I thought I'd tell Lou—" he turned then, to look at Lou's pale face—"There's no news, no sign. We went out as far as we could before the fog started coming in too thick. I thought you might be wondering."

Lou nodded her head.

"I'm sure Mr. Hatch would like some hot cocoa, to warm him before he goes back outside," Mother suggested. She was still standing with the telegram in her hand. Clothilde just sat quiet in her chair, the cloak spread out like a black blanket over her knees. Telegrams carried urgent news, bad news.

"Would you like that, Tom?" Lou asked.

"I'd like it fine, " he said. "I could use a warm drink."

When they had gone into the kitchen, Mother sat down. She folded her needlework neatly onto the table. She opened the yellow envelope with careful fingers, then pulled out the folded flimsy paper, with the strips of words glued onto it.

Mother took a long time reading. The message was only one line long, as Clothilde could see by staring at the back of the paper. Mother read it.

"It's from your grandfather," she said, at last.

"Grandfather? What's the matter? Why should he send us a telegram? What does it say? Mother, tell me."

Instead of answering, Mother passed over the paper. Clothilde read: NATHANIEL HAS COME TO LIVE AT HOME STOP PERMANENTLY STOP AGSPEER . She read it again, as if she couldn't understand what it said. But she understood.

"Nate was lying," she said to her mother. "It was all a lie, about the cruise, and the friends who wanted him to come, wasn't it." She felt too sad to be angry. She never thought Nate would lie to them that way, and it was all somehow her grandfather's doing. "I hate him," she said, thinking of Grandfather.

"You mustn't hate your brother," Mother said. Her hands were back at work, the needle drawing its bright yellow tail behind it, as if nothing had happened.

Clothilde didn't bother correcting her mother's mistake. She pushed the cloak off of her lap, letting it fall onto the floor. She got up and went over to pull aside the curtain. Foggy darkness closed around the house. From the kitchen, she heard Tom Hatch's voice, speaking slowly. She thought of how Grandfather had set about his plan to take Nate away from them, by sending him to a fancy school, buying him good clothes, letting him live in the big house in Manfield. Grandfather's plan had worked and now he had Nate. Ugly, it was an ugly thing Grandfather had done to them. She turned around and looked at her mother's profile. "It's ugly," she said.

"Don't be so quick to judge what you might not understand, Clothilde," her mother answered. But she didn't look up. "You're only a child."

Mother didn't understand at all, but Clothilde didn't want to explain. She hadn't thought how her mother must feel about this, how it might feel to have your son go away from home and never want to come back again. Now she thought of that.

"I'm sorry," she said, meaning sorry that Mother was being made unhappy.

Mother didn't understand this, either. "I'm glad to hear it, and I hope you'll strive to do something to correct that habit of judging other people. Sit down, dear. You've got a task to accomplish. You mustn't be so excitable."

Clothilde sat down, not because she thought she was being excitable, and not because she wanted to finish her task. She sat down so as not to cross her mother. She picked up the cloak and lay it across her knees again. Her fingers began their patient picking out of the stitches, because that was what Mother wanted.

Poor Mother—Grandfather had always been her enemy and now he'd won Nate over to his side. Clothilde thought of how Nate had looked, telling them about the cruise, lying to them. Grandfather had turned Nate into a liar.

But that wasn't it. What it was was worse than that. It was so much worse—and it was why she kept hating Grandfather. Because it was Nate who'd turned himself into a liar. Grandfather just tempted him, with the big house and the clothes, with the factory to inherit and the kind of life where you could have all the things you wanted, with going to boarding school. Nate was tempted. What you did when you were tempted was up to you.

"He should have told us," she said to her mother. "Whatever you say, he should have."

Mother couldn't think of any answer to that, and Clothilde was immediately sorry she'd spoken.

"Anyway, he should have told *you* the truth."

"I'm sure your brother feels unhappy enough about it," Mother said. "That's probably why he didn't tell me. Boys don't like saying unhappy things. Men don't. Nate probably didn't want to hurt my feelings," Mother explained.

Clothilde opened her mouth to protest, but stopped herself from speaking.

"And I'm relieved—no, that's true, dear. I didn't like to

think of him out at sea for such a long time. I didn't want to say anything, but—you never know what might happen. People treat it like a holiday, but a cruise can be dangerous. I'm glad to know he's somewhere safe," Mother said.

"Why didn't you tell him?" Clothilde wondered.

"Oh, he didn't want me worrying at him. Boys like to have their adventures. It's part of their growing up. If mothers worry, they should keep that to themselves."

Clothilde would have asked about that, since Mother seemed to be in the mood to answer questions, but she had just then remembered, once again, her strange dream. She'd gotten one of the things she'd asked for, and she hadn't even noticed: because Nate wasn't going away on the cruise. It wasn't what she'd wanted but it was what she'd asked for.

Clothilde didn't want her dream to be true. She especially didn't want it to be true if you got what you asked for in some twisted way. She hoped it was just a peculiar dream. "Mother, remember that story you told us, about the French girl, Joan?"

"Jeanne," Mother corrected her. "Jeanne d'Arc." One of the orphanage nuns had been French, so Mother had learned how to read and speak French in their school. Even the aunts had to admit she knew that, when they asked her how to pronounce the name of some fancy dish, or a new fabric.

"That girl heard voices, didn't she?"

"Yes, you remember. Whatever brought her into your mind?"

"It wasn't just one voice."

"No, it was voices. Remember? She was told to lead her people in battle, to free the dauphin and crown him. She did those things, remember?"

Clothilde remembered. She remembered also what had happened to the girl, in the end. "Did anyone ever hear just one voice?"

"What odd thoughts you have, Clothilde. I can't answer

that, dear. My schooling wasn't complete. You'd have to ask your father something like that."

"But he—" Again, Clothilde stopped herself; the aunts had often chided Mother because Father hadn't finished school, as if that were her fault.

"We must hope," Mother said gently, "that some day he'll want to come back to live with us."

"No, I didn't mean that." Clothilde didn't want to talk about that. She didn't even want to think about the man in the boathouse. "I meant, Grandfather said he was expelled from school."

"Oh," Mother said. She looked at Clothilde as if she was deciding something. In the hallway, Lou saw Tom Hatch to the door, but neither of them entered the parlor. "You'd have to know sometime," Mother said, "but I don't know that this is the time."

"Know what? What don't I know? *Mother.*" Mother didn't know what to do, Clothilde could see that. So she tried to make her mother do what she, Clothilde, wanted, by sounding sure. "I ought to know."

"The truth is, your father was asked to leave school because he was married to me. The students weren't permitted to be married, that was the rule. But he studied there for almost two years, before, so he learned a great deal. I went to work at fourteen, so I haven't much schooling."

Clothilde could barely remember what her question was, she was so surprised at this new information. "I thought you ran away to get married."

Mother answered quickly. "I had no family. Your grandfather would have tried to stop it, if he'd known. Your father said it would be safer to present him—them—with the thing already done, so it would be too late for them to do anything to stop us. As things turned out, I think that just made it worse, but how was Father to know that? Your father made an adventure of it. He enjoyed the scheming, thinking how he was tricking your grandfather. But he was surprised, and disappointed, when he was asked to leave the college. He didn't think they would really do that."

"But if it was the rule—he must have known the rule."

"Rules are sometimes changed, for special cases. Rules can be broken, I'm afraid. He hoped they would pretend not to know. It was a foolish hope, but . . . how was your father to know?"

"So what happened?"

"As you know, we went to live in Grandfather's house. I didn't want to, but I didn't want to hurt your father any more than I already had."

"How did you hurt him?"

"I shouldn't have agreed to marry him," Mother said, as if it were the most sensible thing in the world. "I don't know how it happened. You see, I thought at first—he was just one of the college boys, the way they flirt and—he was so handsome, and he was always happy—I did say no to him, over and over. But he kept on asking. And I wanted to say yes. Oh—I've never wanted anything like I wanted to say yes. So—I finally did. I'm nothing, nobody, and he gave me so much. . . ." Remembering, she looked up and smiled at Clothilde, but not really seeing her, as if she were looking at somebody who wasn't there. "He came courting me—*me*—with his hands full of candy and flowers, he made me laugh and he offered me his heart. I gave him a son, I did do that. And maybe your grandfather will be satisfied now."

"What do you mean?" Clothilde demanded. "You mean, now he has Nate?"

"Mr. Speer blamed me, for taking Father away from them. They all blamed me, as if I'd enchanted him."

"But you didn't. You couldn't help it if he wanted to marry you."

"I tried, I tried as hard as I could, to be the kind of girl he should have married, the kind they wanted him to marry.

I only wanted him to be happy. I tried not to make him sorry he'd married me, but I'm afraid he was sorry. He couldn't help it."

"Great-Aunt Clothilde must have liked you." Clothilde wanted that to be true.

Mother smiled, but it was the kind of smile grown-ups wear when children just don't know. "She never even noticed me."

Mother wasn't even looking at Clothilde; she wasn't even thinking about her. "I was certain he'd die, when he—went away. I didn't want him to die, and I prayed he wouldn't, but I thought he would. I knew—I shouldn't have flirted with him the way I did, but I never dreamed he was more than one of the college boys. Flirting can be dangerous," Mother warned. "You don't ever want to become a flirt, Clothilde."

"Yes, Mother," Clothilde answered, since her mother was waiting for an answer.

"And now, now I'm afraid he wishes that he *had* died. Over there. Before he went, he was sorry he'd married me. And now, he's . . ."

"Like a monster," Clothilde finished the sentence.

"You mustn't say that," Mother told her. And why not, Clothilde wondered silently, since it was true. "You should be more merciful, Clothilde, in your thoughts. You go right upstairs, right now, go to bed, and pray for more mercy in your heart."

Clothilde didn't know why Mother was so cross at her, and she couldn't make any sense out of their conversation, as if Mother didn't know what she was saying half of the time, and didn't know what she meant the other half. On the other hand, Clothilde was glad to be sent upstairs. She wanted to be alone.

In bed, with the blankets over her and the lamp out, Clothilde tried to reassure herself. People heard voices, not one single voice. Probably, Lou's father would turn up tomorrow or the next day, mean from drinking. She hoped he would. She was angry and sorry that Nate had run away to Grandfather's house, but she couldn't be blamed for that; and it wasn't possible for the man in the boathouse to have his face mended, because that would be a miracle. She didn't want to be responsible for all the things that were happening, and it wasn't possible that she was: She just wasn't that important.

Her mind went around in circles. She stopped its spinning by concentrating on the sound of the slow rain, dripping onto the roof over her head. She thought of Tom Hatch, his kindness in coming out to tell Lou what news there was, and the rain plopped lazily down. Then she thought of Jeb Twohey, and what he'd said about things that grew up and things that grew down. She could bet that Jeb Twohey liked the rain. She thought, her mind drifting now, toward sleep, that Jeb Twohey probably felt safer with plants than with people, and she didn't blame him one bit. She felt that way herself, she thought, falling asleep between the fall of one raindrop and the next.

10

EARLY Tuesday morning, her stomach full with warm oatmeal, Clothilde went to work on the vegetable garden. Wearing an old stained apron over a skirt that was full of its own old stains, she crouched down beside the young chard plants. Her hands, fingers working deep into the water-loosened soil, were eager and full of hope. She didn't understand it, but her heart was full of hope.

The morning was like a spring morning, warm with promises. Nate had not, as it turned out, gone off on his cruise. So that, it might be that the man in the boathouse—

Clothilde wanted to go over there, to see if may-be. . . . She didn't even know what she wanted to be true, but she remembered the way Father would build towers out of blocks, when she was little, and how he would laugh with her when she kicked them down. She let herself remember how once, after the hunt, Mother lifted her up high and Father reached down to carry her up higher, seating her close in front of him on Bucephalus. She rode there all the way down to the stables. She could feel her father's smile all the way, like sunlight coming from behind. He had put the reins into her hands and wrapped his own hands around hers to hold them steady. He had shown her how to run the reins over her two middle fingers. "Gentle and firm," he had said, "that's the way, Clothilde." Remembering, Clothilde missed her father, with a sad longing feeling like the force that pulled the water away out into the deep sea. *Oh,* she thought, her fingers clearing the space around a young plant. *Oh,* she hoped.

Dampness from the ground seeped gradually through her apron and skirt to her knees. The air swept gently around her, full of the smells of the rain-soaked ground. She finished the row of chard and moved over to the bush beans. Overhead the sky was covered by fat gray clouds, moving patiently along. When Mother called to her from the kitchen door, Clothilde was almost sorry to cease working. But she obeyed the call, content to be obedient.

Mother had made the creamed chicken. While Lou scrubbed the wooden floors upstairs, Mother had stripped the poached fowl of its meat, then cut the meat into big chunks. She had made a light creamy sauce, the aroma of which was still in the air, creamy and buttery, with a faint smell of sweet nutmeg. She held out a dish filled with fresh-boiled white rice and thick creamed chicken. "I want you to take this over to the boathouse, dear," Mother said, covering the dish with a cloth.

Mother had covered her dress with an apron while she cooked, but now she took the apron off and washed her hands at the sink, as if trying to wash away any signs of cooking.

Clothilde held the bowl in her two hands. "Why don't you take it?" she asked.

"He doesn't like to see me. He probably won't be there. He won't ask you in."

"But—" Clothilde said. One look at Mother's face stopped her words in her throat.

"I don't want to hear any more from you, young lady."

But that wasn't what Clothilde had been going to say. She had been going to ask, didn't Mother want the chance to give this to him. If Mother wasn't interested to know what Clothilde was really going to say, then Clothilde wasn't going to argue. She did want to be the one to go to the boathouse, and maybe the one to bring him back home because he had been made better.

"Yes, Mother," she said.

"You needn't worry. He doesn't try to talk."

"But you said—you told us he told you we had to save money. How could he tell you that if he doesn't talk?"

"That time—then—he didn't allow me to come in. I was standing outside. You're becoming a quarrelsome person, Clothilde," Mother said. "I don't have the time or patience for this quarreling."

"Yes, Mother," Clothilde said.

"And I don't care for that tone of voice, Clothilde," Mother said. "I'd like to hear you speak more respectfully."

Clothilde nodded her head, but didn't trust herself to speak. It wasn't disrespect that had been in her voice, it was puzzlement. She thought of Mother dressing up fine in hat and gloves to walk over to the boathouse. She wondered why Mother had done that, if the man wasn't going to be there. She wondered why Mother kept thinking she knew what Clothilde was thinking when she didn't have any idea. She wondered why Mother didn't know that it wasn't that the man didn't want to see *her*, all prettied up, but that he didn't want her to see him, the way he looked.

Clothilde washed her hands, picked up the covered dish, and went on her way. Cutting straight across the peninsula, she made her approach along the broad, once-graveled driveway, between the tall spruce trees where Great-Aunt Clothilde's high-wheeled carriages had once rolled. Because of carrying the bowl, she had to keep her feet moving slowly, but her thoughts ran on ahead.

The ruins of the burned cottage were at the top of a slow rise of land. She barely had time to see them before she turned down the slope, along an overgrown path. The boathouse had been built out on the rocks beyond what had once been a lawn. The boathouse had never been intended to hold boats of any size. It was one room, she knew, from peeking in through its grimy windows, where dinghies and oars and sails could be stored. Its shingles had never been stained, so they had weathered to a gray as soft as the clouds overhead. When she had been there before, exploring her peninsula, she hadn't spent much time on the boathouse. It looked as if it were being torn apart by weather. You could almost see the stages by which it would eventually collapse into a huddle of boards and shingles on the broad rocks. The steps that led from the little building across the rocks and down to deep water were askew, most loosened, some of them hanging down. The railing, she remembered, had been as rickety as it looked—the kind of railing that was more dangerous than no railing, because you were tempted to rest your hand and your faith on it. Clothilde followed the path down to the boathouse, wondering what it would look like, now it was inhabited.

Except that the windows had been brushed free of cobwebs, it looked the same. The stairway still careered wildly over the rocks. Parts of the railing had fallen off, to leave blank spaces in the line. The boathouse looked abandoned, as if it wanted to fall apart and be done with enduring. Clothilde, now she was actually there, hesitated. She thought that if she'd thought about it, what she saw was just what she would have expected.

Turning, she looked behind her, up the grassy slope to where blackened beams rose up out of the rubble, like pointing fingers, as if they wanted to accuse the sky. The boathouse sat under the shadow of that destroyed cottage, lived in its shadow. Under that constant reminder of destruction, the boathouse couldn't forget.

Clothilde went up and knocked on the sagging door. No voice answered her. There was no sound from within. The only sound was the slapping of water up against the rocks.

That familiar sound made the silence from within the building more strange.

She could almost see the man, crouched in there. He would be barely breathing, to make no noise. He would have raised his head to look at the door. If you were inside, there was no way out except the one door, so he was trapped, and he felt that. His only hope was silence and stillness.

Clothilde knocked again. She held the covered bowl up close against her stomach, to keep it secure while her right hand was rapping on the wood. Again, no answer.

Mother would have stood there, waiting for an answer. Mother would stand and wait, for a long time, maybe calling out once or twice. Then she would set the bowl down on the peeling wooden stoop and make her slow way back to the farmhouse, her long skirts brushing against the grass.

Clothilde knocked again—sometimes, the third time was a charm. She rapped with her bare knuckles against the wood. Mother's knocking would sound different, she thought; the man inside would know it wasn't Mother. Even so, there was once again no answer.

She wasn't like Mother, and she was getting cross, cross and impatient. She felt sorry for anyone who huddled away, too frightened to open the door, but that wasn't going to stop her. Clothilde turned the metal knob and pushed at the door.

The door scraped against the wooden floor, trying to stick, but she forced it open. The one room was dimly lit by three high windows; shadows crowded against what little light came in. The room was empty.

Clothilde stood in the open door, looking around: nobody sat on the bedroll, nobody crouched in the corners. A pile of clothes lay like old rags on the floor by the bedroll. A painted table was set in the middle of the room, but there was no chair. A wooden box had been placed on its end to hold an enamel bowl, the kind you used in a sickroom, and some pieces of paper had been stuck on the walls with nails. One long wooden plank made a shelf along the length of the room; on that was a messkit, a metal mug, a glass jar half full of clear liquid—water, probably, but where did he get his water from? At the other end of the shelf was a narrow wooden box, the size of a music box, on top of pads of drawing paper.

What a dismal place it was. She moved to set the covered bowl down on the table, at the center of the table like a bowl of flowers, to cheer up the room. Then she stood, looking around.

He would wash in the enamel bowl, she thought. There was no sign of any fire, or stove to cook on, so she guessed he would go outside and bring in cold sea water for washing. She guessed he would eat cold food. A kerosene lamp on the floor beneath a window must be his only light, during the long dark hours; he would wrap himself up in one of the blankets thrown over the bedroll, and sit by the lamp. There were no books on the shelves and she wondered how he passed those long dark hours. He had made no effort to make the room comfortable.

Clothilde walked around, imagining what it would be like to live there. Spots on the wooden floor showed where the roof had leaked during the night's rain. The room was damp, and chilly. She moved around, and approached one of the pieces of paper, high on the wall. It was a drawing, done in dark pencil, or maybe charcoal. The paper had been ripped out of a pad, ripped carelessly.

She went closer and saw that it was a landscape, distant and barren. All the lines were dark. She wondered if the lines had been done in ink, they were so clear and black. A crumbled building with one tower left standing lay at the distant horizon, and odd wavy lines ran across the ground until a shapeless dark mass took over, spreading out from the bottom right-hand corner. It was cold there, maybe in some icy country, Greenland or Finland or Siberia. She didn't know how she knew how cold it was, just as she didn't know how she knew that it was daytime, and the sun was bright somewhere over her shoulder if she was in the picture. She didn't stay long in front of it, it was so cold and dead, but went to look at the picture above the basin.

That one she recognized—it was his face, a pencil sketch of that monster face, tacked up where a mirror should be. She looked back at the landscape, and saw now what the dark mass of color was—shadows. Going up close to it again, she could pick out shadows of men, with rounded metal helmets on their heads, elongated on that frozen ground. When she looked, she could see that some of the shadows did not have living men behind them, and she could see how very many men were there. One shadow blended into the other so completely, they crowded their section of the picture.

Horrible, it was a horrible drawing. Clothilde wanted to rip it down from the wall and rip it into pieces. But it wasn't hers, so she didn't. It belonged to that face over the washbasin.

Before he might return Clothilde left the boathouse, pulling the door closed behind her. Outside, she hesitated, breathing in the sweet wet air and rubbing her hands on her apron, as if she wanted to clean them off.

She looked down into the rocky cove. No one. Only the water, gurgling, lifting its heavy burden of seaweed, up and down, as it rose and fell with the waves.

The landscape on the wall—Clothilde had once slipped along a weedy rock and slid down, falling into the water. The water had closed over her head, enveloping her. The water had been icy cold and she felt, rising back to the surface, how completely it surrounded her, how it soaked its coldness into her skin and into her heart. She could swim a little, so she wasn't frightened. It wasn't fear that had set her heart racing and made her gasp for air when she emerged, even though she hadn't been underwater long at all. It wasn't fear she had felt, feeling her feet slip out from under her and her slow, helpless sliding down the rock. She never knew what it was, but she recognized it in that barren landscape.

Keeping her eyes on the ground because she couldn't bear, at that moment, to see the ruined cottage, Clothilde crossed quickly into the woods. Instead of heading back to the farmhouse and her unfinished chores, she turned east and made her way through the pathless woods to the headlands. Her head was full of so many things at once—ideas leaped out at her, snapping across her mind the way branches slapped at her face and arms. He didn't have a mirror, she thought; and nothing had been done to make the boathouse comfortable. Jeb Twohey's empty eyes, and Polly Dethier's eyes lit up with so much hope that it must hurt her to hope so much. Those shadows, massed together in a black shape—none of them had guns, no weapons, just the round helmets to protect them. The sky overhead, the way light warmed the air and glowed behind the high soft cloud cover. In that landscape—nothing growing, and no color. Nothing reaching up that loved sunlight, everything downward, loving rain, if Jeb Twohey's words made any sense. If Dierdre, just a little child, looked at you and screamed. With no mirror, if there were any change, any healing, he wouldn't see it.

Out on the headlands, she climbed down the rocks—placing her feet carefully, avoiding slippery patches of seaweed—climbing down to meet the water. The tide had just turned from the high. She crouched at the edge of a rock, looking down through the clear water to the rocks piled up below, underwater, with their dark crevices the water stole into. Then she looked out, away to the unbroken water beyond the little islands where they lay under the pillowy gray sky. From a distance, the water looked like a blanket, a rumpled blanket woven of dark blues and grays.

Nearby, three black cormorants swam along the shore. As she watched, one after the other they dove. Watching, waiting, she saw them resurface, at a distance. They popped up from underwater like floats, then resumed their sedate paddling. They were three black shapes, almost like cutouts, with narrow curved necks. They were there, and then gone.

Clothilde knew she had to get back home, so she turned. Turning, she saw the figure of a man on top of the next headland. He hadn't seen her. He was looking the other way. What she saw was his back, the high-necked white sweater he wore, the trousers that seemed too big for him, the heavy boots. She crawled back up over the rocks, hoping he wouldn't turn and see her. When she got to the top, she stared across at the figure for a minute, wondering—if he turned—if she would see new skin growing over his face. The creamed chicken would be cold by the time he came to eat it. The rice would be stuck together in gummy clumps.

When he did turn around, she wanted to run away but made herself stay still, hoping to blend into the trees behind her. He had no idea anyone was there and his body froze stiff in surprise. It only took a second before he had disappeared abruptly into the concealing trees. It only took a second or two, and she was too far away to see well, but she could see there was no difference in the face. She knew, just before he turned away, that she'd been staring, so she raised her hand—and he turned away.

Clothilde, going back to her chores by way of her own path through the woods to the beach, didn't know if she was disappointed or relieved. Just because Nate hadn't gone cruising didn't mean her dream was true. If she'd known the kind of lies Nate had been telling, she would have guessed that this cruise was another lie. She would have guessed that he'd go live with Grandfather because—looked at a certain way—that was the only sensible thing to do. There was nothing like magic going on, or wishes coming true. If she'd been a boy, she might have done just what Nate did. It didn't take any voices to make Nate do that. As if any Voice would come just to ask Clothilde what she wanted. How childish could you be, like Dierdre afraid of ghosts, believing in fairy godmothers. When she thought of the hope she had started out the morning with—Clothilde could have laughed at herself.

11

MOTHER met Clothilde at the door with news: "He's been found," she said. "They've both been found."

Clothilde wondered for a minute, Who did she know who was lost? Then, "Mr. Small," she said. She wasn't surprised. It made sense for Nate to run away to Grandfather; so if he hadn't gone on that cruise, there wasn't anything too strange about it. The man in the boathouse wouldn't have turned away from her if he had put his hand to his face—the way you often did, every day—and felt healing on his skin; so healing wasn't happening. "And Mr. Twohey. I'm glad. Where were they?"

Mother spoke sternly. "They were both drowned, Clothilde. I've put Dierdre to bed."

"Why?" Clothilde asked stupidly. She couldn't think why Mother should put Dierdre to bed at this hour of the afternoon.

"Nobody knows," Mother answered. "There's no sign of their boat."

"Oh no," Clothilde said. But it was true, and she knew it.

"Do you need to go to your room, for a rest?"

Clothilde shook her head. The last place she wanted to be was in bed, where all she could do was think. She felt

113

strange. She felt as if she were miles away from the person who just stood staring at Mother.

"It may be for the best," Mother said. "Sometimes, it's better this way."

"Don't say that, Mother."

Mother's lips closed tight. "Girls are not to speak in that tone of voice to any adult, especially their parents. Mr. Small was not a good father. You are too young to understand what that means, but his death may well prove a blessing to his family."

Clothilde shook her head. She didn't want it to be true that Mr. Small was dead.

"It's easier for his family this way, dear. It's easier to know what's happened, than to wait—waiting and wondering."

"No," Clothilde said. If you were waiting and wondering, then at least you could hope.

"Lou has gone home. Mr. Dethier gave Tom Hatch the use of his wagon, to come out and fetch her home. That was kind, wasn't it? Often, people can be kind, in times of need. People you least expect it of. Her mother will need Lou with her. But I don't know how we'll manage without her."

"I'll make a pot of tea," Clothilde decided. She would make a pot of tea, boiling the water in the kettle, steeping the leaves in the round white pot. She would set out a tray, with a napkin underneath it, and a little pitcher of milk, two cups, the sugar bowl, and she mustn't forget the spoons. Her body got busy with that.

That night, with Mother and Dierdre deep in sleep, Clothilde climbed out of her bed. She wrapped a blanket over her nightclothes and went quietly down the stairs, silently out the kitchen door. The house was dark, its air filled with sleep, as if she could hear their steady breathing, as if the house itself breathed quietly in sleep. Clothilde couldn't sleep.

She went across the grass to the beach. Her feet were cold, but so was her whole body. She had been cold, numbed, all day—so that now it felt as if her spirit were huddled so deep within her body that it came nowhere near the edges of her flesh. The wind, coming from behind her, blew the long blanket ahead of her. It tangled at her bare feet, but she didn't notice that; the wind was warmer, warmed by the vast inland forests and fields, but she didn't notice that either. On the beach, she couldn't see into the black water, blown up into waves that headed out to the darker ocean. She didn't know what time it was.

Clothilde sat on a flat stone, far back from the water's edge. She drew her feet up under the blanket and stared.

Overhead, the black sky poured forth stars. The waves rushed at the shore and the offshore wind blew them back to where they had come from. Clothilde sat, huddled in her misery.

She hadn't meant that and the Voice knew it. She didn't mean Mr. Small to die, she'd never even thought of that. The Voice should have known what she didn't mean. She hadn't meant dying to happen.

Looking over the water, with the starry sky overhead, she thought of those two bodies floating in. Black shapes on the black water, their backs to the sky. She couldn't even remember what either of the two men looked like, and that was terrible too. If the bodies turned over, she couldn't even identify them. She'd never seen Mr. Small, except maybe a few times, years ago, when he'd been around the farmhouse. Her memory had no picture of him. She should at least remember what he looked like. When she thought of Mr. Twohey, all she could see was Jeb's blank face, but she should know what Mr. Twohey looked like, too. He hadn't even been in what she asked for. He had nothing to do with it.

She was so sorry, she would have taken back everything if she'd been able to. She'd have turned back the clock to

Saturday afternoon and if the Voice came after her, she wouldn't have said anything. She wouldn't have asked for anything. She wished she hadn't asked for anything.

It was as if the Voice had deliberately misunderstood her, as if the Voice had done this to teach her a lesson. It was all a trick. The Voice wanted to trick her. She wondered if the Voice had a good time, filling people with hope, and then tricking them. She wished she had that Voice there, right then, because she would give it an earful. There were some things she'd like to say to that Voice.

And she could just imagine what the Voice had in mind for the man in the boathouse—the exact opposite of what she'd had in mind when she asked. She couldn't imagine what was going to happen to that man, and she was sorry already for him. It was her doing, after all. Whatever she'd meant to do, what she had asked for was what happened.

It wasn't Lou's family she really felt worst about, though, it was Jeb Twohey and his mother, Mr. Twohey's family. They hadn't even been in her mind at all, and they still had to be part of it. She hadn't even thought—

The Voice didn't play fair. The Voice was so big, and powerful, and tricky, it hadn't even told her it might not play fair with her.

She couldn't imagine all that trickiness—the man in the boathouse would have something terrible happen to him, because there was no way to heal his face—and besides, the Voice wasn't about to do what Clothilde really meant—but before whatever it was going to be had happened, the man would sell the peninsula—she was willing to bet on that. That would be the one perfectly true thing the Voice told her, about the peninsula not being hers.

Clothilde looked up, angry. She had a right to be angry, she silently told the stars, burning so whitely out there, safe in the sky. She did, and they knew it.

If they did know it, they didn't care. And even if she did

have a right to be angry, and was angry, she was still so sorry, and ashamed, and—

Clothilde wished—her eyes filled with so many stars you could go crazy trying to count them, her ears filled with the dark wind blowing at her back—she wished she could be as far away from what she'd done as the stars were. Nobody would know to blame her, but she knew she was to blame.

Maybe she would find a way to study to become an astronomer and just look at the stars all her life. Astronomers were awake at night, when everybody else was asleep. But she didn't think girls could be astronomers; there was something about a girl's brain that made that impossible. Like it was impossible for girls to run businesses, like Grandfather's factory. There were things that boys, or men, could understand automatically. She wished she had been born a boy. Boys seemed to know things. Life was easier, because there were more things for boys to choose from. If she had been the one to run away to Grandfather's house, for example, he wouldn't even have let her in the door. He'd have slammed the door in her face if it had been her. If she'd been a boy, she would have seen that there was a trick in it; she was willing to bet on that. She wouldn't have left room for those tricks, if she'd seen. It was impossible, but she wished she'd been born a boy; it was really stupid, but she was angry at herself about that, too, as angry as she was at herself about what she'd asked the Voice for.

She hadn't meant to hurt the Twoheys. She hadn't even meant to hurt Mr. Small. She'd meant only to make things better, and that was about the opposite of what had happened. She'd thought it would be so simple, she'd thought things were so simple, and she was wrong. She couldn't even trust herself.

12

EMPTY-HANDED, Clothilde entered the empty church. Nobody would be in there on a Wednesday afternoon. She hadn't come to pray. It was only habit that made her sit down at the end of the row of wooden seats, and it wasn't praying when she bowed her head. After the night's regret and a morning's thought, she had come to stop the Voice before it did any more terrible things.

She no longer felt huddled away somewhere deep inside her body. She felt as if her body itself had shrunk up, over the night and the long morning, to fit close around her huddled self. She felt like one of the drowned worms that lay at the road's edges after a long rain—a bloated twisted brown thing. An ugly thing.

Clothilde bent her head lower and put her arms up beside her head, twining her fingers together behind her neck. She made herself sick to her stomach.

She hadn't slept much—maybe that was it, what made her feel so very bad; she hadn't eaten much because her stomach seemed to close up at the thought of food. She had gotten out of bed early, prepared breakfast for her mother and sister, washed the kitchen floor and then, under her mother's orders, she had baked a coffeecake. "You should pay a condolence call on Lou and her family," Mother had said.

"Why not you?"

"That wouldn't be appropriate. I will send in the cake, and a message of sympathy. Don't fidget so, Clothilde, I can't get these braids done properly it you fidget. And don't always be quarreling and fussing at me—it would only embarrass the poor woman if I were to go calling on her."

Clothilde didn't know about that; she didn't know about anything. She had mixed and kneaded the sweet dough; before the second rising, she had scattered sugar and currants over the top of it. She had baked it, let it cool, set it out on a good platter—"But not the best, Clothilde, that would embarrass the poor woman." She had the cake covered with a clean cloth and walked through the warm summer noonday into the village. The sun, pouring down from a clear sky, hadn't warmed her. The walk hadn't tired her. She hadn't come into the church to rest in its shady coolness. And she certainly hadn't come to pray, at least not until the Voice had explained itself.

That thought raised her head. Worm or not, there were some questions she wanted to ask, and some answers she thought she was owed. This whole thing should be stopped, to start with.

Silence filled the church. *Come on*, Clothilde thought. *Come out*. The church was a single room. It wasn't large enough for a center aisle, but the high vaulted ceiling gave it a sense of space. *I'm here, I'm waiting*.

The floors were made of broad pine planks, the walls of narrow pine planks, the seats and altar and pulpit too, all were made from the same pine. The wood had aged to a deep golden color, the wood floor, the wood walls, and the wood ceiling overhead. Even the narrow arches that floated between wall and ceiling glowed woody gold. It was like being inside of a tree, being in that church.

Light entered through long stained-glass windows, filling

the air with the echoes of colors like the echoes of voices. Clothilde looked at the newest window, installed less than a year ago. The whole congregation, which was everyone in the village, had contributed to its cost, and Mr. Dethier had made up whatever more money was needed. They had wanted their own war-memorial window. They had ordered it from a Boston company that specialized in war memorials. On the window, a tall woman in a white robe held out a sword in one hand and a wreath in the other. She was the Republic. Under her feet were a list of names, in two columns, names of the men in the village who had fought in the war. The list was not long; it was a small village. Clothilde knew all of those men, knew who they were. Tom Hatch, Alexander Hatch, Jeb Twohey, Robert Dethier, Benjamin F. Speer II, Thomas Henderson, John Henderson. Of the seven boys, two had never returned, and three—the Henderson boys and Tom Hatch—had come back without a scratch on them.

The names were painted onto a scroll that unrolled under the bare feet of the Republic. The Twoheys had refused to make any contribution to the window. This made people angry, but Clothilde felt a secret sympathy for the Twoheys. She had given in the few pennies she had, but if they asked her now . . . she'd probably give pennies if she had them, she guessed, but she wouldn't *want* to donate anything, and she might be brave enough to refuse.

And where was the Voice, anyway? It was probably laughing at her somewhere, expecting her to sit there all day.

She got up, took a last look around her at the wooden walls and the motes floating in the air, and left. She pulled the wooden door loudly closed behind her, picking up her platter from the long table in the foyer.

The blacksmith's shop was across the street and, built out behind it, the two-room house Lou's family rented. One end of the little house leaned up against the tall red side of the blacksmith's barn and a narrow stovepipe came out of its roof. Curtains were closed over the two windows, and a black wreath hung on the door. Clothilde knocked and was told to come on in.

Mrs. Grindle sat at the table, as did Mrs. Henderson and Mrs. Small. Lou stood with her back to the room, washing dishes in a pan, and noises from the next room told Clothilde where Lou's brothers and sisters were. A big cast-iron teapot steamed on the pot-bellied stove. A red-and-white checked oilcloth had been spread out over the table.

As soon as Clothilde was inside, Mrs. Henderson rose. "I have to be going now. Mr. Henderson is expecting me," she said. She wore a black shawl around her shoulders, pinned together with a cameo brooch. She had kept the shawl on over her white blouse, despite the heat in the closed room.

Mrs. Small got up to walk Mrs. Henderson the few paces to the door. "We thank you for your kindness. We also thank you for the chicken pie."

"Oh, I thought you wouldn't be up to cooking, and I know that whatever happens, children have to be fed. It's little enough to do, when a neighbor has troubles."

After Mrs. Henderson had left, Mrs. Small turned to Clothilde. "Good afternoon, Miss Clothilde," she said. Mrs. Small was as pale as Lou, and as thin in her bones, but she had gone fat all around them. Her black dress made her look all the paler, but she didn't seem gloomy, despite her black dress and solemn expression.

"Mother asked me to tell you how sorry she is," Clothilde began. "For your trouble," she added.

"Your mother is a real lady," Mrs. Small said, then waited for what Clothilde was supposed to say next.

Clothilde didn't know what she was supposed to say. She felt like a worm saying anything, and being there too. She thrust the covered cake at Mrs. Small. "This is for you."

"How kind of your mother. Sweet cake is such a comfort.

Lou? Set a clean plate for Miss Clothilde. Will you sit down, miss?"

Clothilde sat in the chair Mrs. Henderson had left empty. She nodded hello to Mrs. Grindle, who had a plate in front of her with some kind of fruitcake half-eaten on it.

Nobody said anything. Lou put a plate down in front of Clothilde and asked if she wanted some tea. Clothilde mumbled her refusal. Lou sliced the coffeecake onto another plate and put that out at the center of the table, removing the fruitcake. Mrs. Small took a slice of Clothilde's cake, bit into it, and smiled at Clothilde.

Wishing she was anywhere else but there, wondering why she had to sit at the table, Clothilde smiled back at Mrs. Small. Looking at the pale eyes, she knew—as if she could see into Mrs. Small's head and see her secret thoughts—that the newly widowed woman wasn't grief-stricken at all.

"We thank you for your trouble," Mrs. Small said at last.

Mrs. Grindle had taken a slice of cake and eaten it. Her little mouth pursed as she chewed. "Is this hard to make?" she asked.

Clothilde shook her head.

"I'd like to have the recipe," Mrs. Grindle said. "If your mother could spare it."

"I'll ask her." Then Clothilde, feeling as if Mrs. Small expected her to say this, said, "I'm sorry for your trouble." But that sounded as if she was speaking lightly of a man's death. "Your loss."

"Life's not been easy on me," Mrs. Small agreed, satisfied. "His was an untimely end."

"Although," Mrs. Grindle said, ignoring Clothilde, "there's a silver lining to this, if you're willing to look for it." It sounded as if Mrs. Grindle was picking up a conversation Clothilde had interrupted.

"He wasn't an easy husband," Mrs. Small agreed.

Mrs. Grindle's mouth made an impatient, pffting noise.

"You can't pretend it's not a blessing. He was dragging you all down with him. Your children will be better off without him. And look what he did to Joseph Twohey."

"You can't lay that at Mr. Small's doorstep," Mrs. Small argued. "Mr. Small had his weakness—I've never denied that and I never will. But Joseph Twohey went to perdition of his own free will."

They talked as if Clothilde weren't there, or as if it didn't matter what she heard. She wished they wouldn't talk so.

"There's free will," Mrs. Grindle said. "And there's the straw that breaks the camel's back. When Jeb came home, the way he is, what was there for Joseph to work for? I was grateful, I'll admit it to you, that our sons were too old and our grandsons too young for this war. I always said that, no matter how people might look sideways at me."

Clothilde hadn't known Mrs. Grindle felt that way about the war. The woman across the table noticed her attention and said, "You needn't bother thinking ill of me, Miss High and Mighty. When you're older you'll understand."

But Clothilde already understood.

Mrs. Grindle went on talking, scolding at Clothilde. "There's a package for your mother. From some Boston store. Some fancy Boston store, for all I've never heard the name. She must have written away for it because it's addressed to Mr. B.F. Speer. You might as well pick it up on your way home—it might be something she's expecting."

Mrs. Grindle waited, but Clothilde couldn't make any guess about what the package might be, so she couldn't satisfy the woman's curiosity.

"And you might tell your mother, as well, that her account's due to be paid up." *If she's fine enough to be ordering things from Boston, she can pay what she owes here in the village* was what Mrs. Grindle didn't say.

Clothilde had to bite the insides of her cheeks to keep from smiling. "Yes, ma'am," she said. This was no place for smiling, and it surely wasn't the time either. She didn't know why she felt like it anyway, except it was either that or burst out and tell them what had really happened, whose fault it really was, even if it wasn't what she'd meant to happen. And anyway, watching Mrs. Grindle's mind, which was as pursed up in disapproval as her lips, made Clothilde feel like laughing.

"You can stop by and pick it up before you go out home," Mrs. Grindle told her. "It's not as if we're a storehouse, it's not as if we have extra space to store people's packages from Boston emporiums."

"No, ma'am," Clothilde said. "I'll fetch Mother's package."

That, however, turned out to be unnecessary, because the next person to arrive was Mr. Grindle, and along with his sympathy for the new widow, he brought the wrapped package for Clothilde. He took the seat Clothilde vacated and handed her the package. "I saw you go past the store," he said to her. "You didn't come straight here."

Clothilde took the long, flat package. It was heavy for its size. She didn't know what her mother had sent away for. She went over to stand beside Lou, to help her if possible, because she didn't know if she had stayed long enough yet. Mr. Grindle's voice told the two women how he had closed the store, "in honor," for the next two hours. He accepted the offer of cake and asked could Lou make a pot of coffee, saying he never could get used to drinking tea, saying it was a sad day for the village. Then he asked, "What is this my wife tells me—you're going to pack up and move back south? To Fall River?"

Clothilde was beside Lou, their backs to the room as Lou poured water from a bucket into the steel coffeepot. "You're leaving the village?" she asked, her voice low. "Don't do that. You don't have to do that. Why would you do that?" That wasn't what she wanted. That wasn't what she'd asked for. She should have asked for money, that's what; money solved everything. Nate would have known to ask for money, but she was too stupid to think of it.

"Yuh, we'll go to my aunt. There's a bed for us, until we can save up for our own rooms," Lou answered. "There's always work at the mills."

"Oh no," Clothilde said. The mills were terrible places— Lou shouldn't have to go back there.

"My mother will be pleased to return. Our own church is there, and her sister, her blood kin."

"You should stay here," Clothilde insisted. "I'm sorry, Lou."

Lou didn't say anything. Thinking of the room Lou had made for herself at the farmhouse, and how contented she had seemed there with them, Clothilde asked, "Maybe you'll come back." She looked at Lou's pale face. Lou looked right back at her: Lou grieved, alone, inside herself, Clothilde could feel that, grieved for what she would be leaving behind, places and people, silences and light; Lou's future pressed down on her like a huge rock, always pressing harder, with a perpetual clattering grinding noise like the mills working. Clothilde didn't know how any one person could stand being pressed down by that weight. Just imagining it made her feel as if she couldn't breathe in enough air to live. "You have to come back," she said.

"I don't think so," Lou said. "But I don't mind thinking mebbe. I'd like it fine, yuh."

Clothilde couldn't do anything more, except be helpful. She dried the plates Lou had washed, and stacked them up. More people arrived, the Grindles left to call on Mrs. Twohey, who was, Mrs. Grindle said, "devastated by this blow," and Clothilde pumped up water into the bucket from the well outside, heated it on the stove, went back outside to empty the dirty dishwater, and did what she could. People brought food and company. They offered help for the move. Mr. Dethier offered his wagon to transport the family to the train station in Ellsworth, Tom Hatch said he would drive them there, and the blacksmith's wife told Mrs. Small not to worry about cleaning out the rooms because she would take care of that little chore. The afternoon wore on, wore away.

It seemed that people went from one bereaved house to the other, because many brought news of the Twohey household, which was a sadder place than this small room. "You have your children," they said to Mrs. Small. "Many hands help bear the burdens."

Tom Hatch stayed the afternoon too, standing back from the talk but lending a hand wherever it was needed, with all the company. It was hot and dim in that little room, and Clothilde, whenever she had cause to step outside, was surprised to find that it was still daylight.

The sun had set before Clothilde left the little house. Tom Hatch had borrowed Mr. Dethier's wagon, so he could take her home. They sat side by side on the wooden seat; the horse, with blinders to keep his eyes fixed on the roadway, pulled them along at a steady pace, through the village and along the fork by the schoolhouse. A lantern, hung at the brace beside Tom Hatch, gave them light.

Clothilde had her mother's package heavy across her knees and guilt heavy across her shoulders. All the windows at the Twoheys' were dark, except for one on the ground floor. The house was a mute, black shape with only that one dim window, where a light burned behind the drawn shades. The lantern cast flickering shadows. The air grew chilly. Clothilde didn't have anything to say as they went along, past the dark meadows and farmlands and over the causeway where the sound of waves on rocks could be heard, punctuated by the horse's steady footsteps.

The wagon moved along the rutted driveway. Overhead, the leafy branches closed in over them, emerging from the darkness ahead, then fading into the darkness behind as the wagon passed. It was like moving through a tunnel. But whether the leafy ceiling overhead was there to keep them safe or to shut them in, Clothilde couldn't tell. Finally, she roused herself to say, "It's kind of you to bring me home, Mr. Hatch."

"I couldn't let you walk the way alone, and in the dark," he said. "Now, could I?"

Yes, she thought, he could have. But he hadn't.

"I wish someone could persuade Lou not to go away. Could you?" she asked him.

"She's a girl yet, and she has to stay with her family besides."

"Her family needs her," Clothilde agreed. "But still—it's not right. She hates the mills. She told me, she hates it there."

"Yuh," he said. "She would."

"Even if she had been going to stay on with us," Clothilde realized, "now she wouldn't be able to anyway."

"Yuh," he agreed, with such hopelessness in his voice she turned to look at him. She wished she hadn't done that, because he had turned to look at her, at the same time, in the wavery yellow lantern light. His eyes were shadowed, but she could still see them, and she turned away. The horse's hooves sounded muffled on the dirt. The wagon bounced along. They moved in an arched doorway of light, under the trees.

Tom Hatch wanted Lou to stay in the village because he wanted to court her, and marry her. Clothilde knew that, although she didn't know how she knew. But Lou was too young yet, he thought, so he hadn't spoken to her. Now Lou would be moving two states away. He would have made a good husband for Lou; Tom Hatch was a good man and a good friend. Lou would have made a good wife. Lou was young in numbered years, but she was old enough. Clothilde opened her mouth to say all this to Tom Hatch, and ask him please to ask Lou: but she closed her mouth before she let a single word out.

Besides, Lou would just say No, if he asked her now.

Lou had to go with her family, because she was the only one old enough to get work.

The light lit the undersides of the leaves growing on the branches of the many trees. Darkness was all around them.

Besides, she might have it all wrong. Who was she, anyway, to think she was so smart about things. She had thought she was so smart before, and so right too, and look what she had done.

13

On Thursday morning, Clothilde was the first to wake. She built a little fire in the parlor, to take the night chill off the air so that when Mother and Dierdre came to sit it would be comfortable. She started a pot of oatmeal and set the table the way Mother wanted it to be set, with plates, napkins, and spoons, the pitcher filled with milk, the sugar bowl filled. Everything was ready when they came down, everything was done the way Mother wanted it done. But all the busyness couldn't stop her thinking: her hands worked but her mind kept on thinking.

It wasn't what she'd wanted. She hadn't even mentioned Mr. Twohey. Mr. Small—and she thought of the way Lou's face had looked that one morning, it was before Lou lived-in with them; Lou had come in that morning with the right side of her face swollen and discolored, as if her face had been caught in the machines and twisted like her hands had been—Mr. Small she had mentioned, and that was why. But she hadn't meant he should die. It was her fault, and it wasn't even what she'd wanted. It certainly wasn't what she'd asked for, either.

When they were through eating, Clothilde washed up the breakfast dishes. She told herself that what had happened had happened and she couldn't undo it. That was funny, she couldn't undo things, she could only do them.

Clothilde mopped the kitchen floor before she went to find Mother. She needed to know what Mother wanted done first, the clothes dampened for ironing or the batch of bread started. If she looked in the mirror, she was afraid she would see a worm there, an ugly thing with its blunt blind head; that was what she should see, even when it wasn't what she did see.

She was so sorry. Even if it wasn't her fault, she was still sorry and she didn't know how she would ever make up for what she'd done. What she'd done wasn't what she was like, but she didn't know how to prove that.

Mother wasn't in the parlor. The brown-wrapped package from Boston waited on the table. Clothilde had given Mother the package, and Mrs. Grindle's message, last night. "I don't know what to do," Mother had said; "I don't know what I'm supposed to do."

"You're supposed to take care of things," Clothilde had reminded her, too worn down to think before she spoke. Mother's eyes had opened wide, and Clothilde was sorry, but she ran upstairs before Mother could speak again.

Mother was probably dressing, to deliver the package to the man in the boathouse. Clothilde went upstairs to find her. It was all right if Mother wanted to look like a lady, and pretend she was a lady; there were worse things than ladies in the world.

But Mother wasn't in her bedroom. Looking out of the window, Clothilde saw the two of them, Mother and Dierdre, in the garden below. Mother was bending over— weeding it looked like. Her hair hung down her back in a plain braid. She wore a plain blouse and skirt, and an apron. Clothilde didn't know what to think.

She stood looking down at them, as if they were a painting. The two figures bent over the earth. Overhead, high thin clouds floated along a sky so blue it could have been some kind of mineral stone, and you could cut it into chunks and sell it for jewelry. It was a good picture, Mother and Dierdre working side by side, in the brown soil of the garden.

Clothilde went outside to ask her question. Mother was teaching Dierdre how to recognize weeds. Clothilde remembered when Mother taught her that; she had been older than Dierdre was, quicker to learn. Dierdre's pile of weeds was awfully small.

"Is this one?" Dierdre asked, her fingers around the delicate stem of a clover. "Mother, is this one?"

Mother turned around to say Yes. She turned back to her work.

"Am I done now?" Dierdre asked. "Mother, am I done?"

Mother turned around to say No, not yet, there's a lot more to do.

Dierdre looked at Mother's back. Clothilde didn't know what her sister was thinking. Dierdre waited a moment, then reached out to pull up a weed.

"Not that one, Dierdre," Clothilde warned her.

Mother straightened up and turned around. "Remember, the ones like ferns are carrots. They're in the straight row, remember?"

Dierdre looked at Clothilde and at Mother. She had to look up for both of them. Clothilde couldn't remember being that little—Dierdre was so little and round, her eyes were so big, you just wanted to make her happy. "I'm hungry," Dierdre said.

"No you aren't, dear," Mother answered, and turned back to her own weeding.

"I am. Am too. Mother? Can I have something to eat?"

Dierdre couldn't be hungry. It wasn't an hour since the good breakfast she'd eaten. Clothilde looked at her sister's round face. The chin was so little and her thick hair didn't want to stay caught in braids. The hand-me-down pinafore she wore was too big for her, so it was tied up across her chest. Her blue eyes looked at Clothilde.

"An apple," she said. "I want an apple. Clothilde could get it."

The eyes were hungry, and the little white teeth between her pouting lips were ready to bite into something. Dierdre was hungry, Clothilde thought, or, at least, she felt as if she was hungry, but it wasn't stomach hunger. It was heart hunger, as if, no matter how much attention and love you gave to her she wouldn't be full. Greedy, Clothilde thought, looking at the little girl who was scowling up at her now, hoping that anger would get her what whining didn't.

"Dierdre," Clothilde warned, when Dierdre reached out to interrupt Mother again. Then she had an idea because she could see—almost as if she were inside of Dierdre's head and walking around—how hard it would be to always be wanting more. She could guess what might soothe her sister. "Dierdre? If you can weed that whole row, without pulling up a single carrot, we'll make an apple pie for supper. You and me."

"Don't know how."

"I can teach you," Clothilde answered. If you needed attention and love, and you couldn't ever give it to yourself . . . then you'd always be asking other people for it. "You're big enough to learn."

"Could I make my own?"

Greedy and selfish, Clothilde thought. But she wasn't so perfect that she had the right to criticize Dierdre, was she? "Your own little pie? Your very own little pie just for you?"

"And roll it out. And prick it with a knife."

"Not a knife, a fork," Clothilde said. "Yes, you can, if you do the whole row. With no carrot mistakes. And not asking Mother every time."

"Easy," Dierdre said. She was smiling now, happy again with something to look forward to.

"Should I start bread rising, or—" Clothilde asked her mother's back.

Once again, Mother turned around. Clothilde felt how Mother was trying to stay patient; and she could understand why, because Clothilde had interrupted her mother's work, just like Dierdre.

"I'm sorry," she said, but Mother spoke at the same time:

"You'll have to take that package over to the boathouse. It's his. He must have ordered it. I hope he paid for it, because. . . ." She wiped her hand across her forehead, as if she could wipe all the worry away. Her hand left a trail of dirt.

"He ought to ask Grandfather for money," Clothilde said. Men were supposed to take care of their families.

"He can't do that, dear. He can't go begging to his father."

"Then he should ask Nate—I bet Nate'll have plenty of spending money now," Clothilde said.

"Or to his son."

Besides, Clothilde thought, look what happened when you started asking for things.

"And bring back the bowl the chicken was in, too, if you would," Mother said.

"But why don't you go?"

Mother shook her head. "Not looking like this. It's better if you do it, dear. Right away, please, so you can gather mussels at low tide, we'll have a stew."

Clothilde wanted to say No. But Mother's face had that streak of dirt across it. So Clothilde nodded her head. She tried to say how much she wished Mother could have things the way she wanted them. "Are we ever going to have flowers growing here?"

"I can't see where we'd find the time, can you?" But Mother smiled at Clothilde and Clothilde wondered how much her mother minded not having flowers after all. Because, she thought suddenly, still nodding like some puppet at her mother, what her mother really wanted was to have things growing, even just beans and chard. Her mother didn't mind work, either. She only minded not knowing what she should do. Mother thought, because she was an orphan—Clothilde unexpectedly saw what it might be, to be an orphan and not somebody who belonged, and if there were somebody who wanted to marry you, even if you were an orphan—but then if you thought he was sorry he'd done that—how would you know what to do? With everyone telling you you weren't good enough, because you weren't anybody.

Clothilde would take the package, but she didn't even remove her apron and she didn't hurry one bit. She carried the wrapped parcel under one arm as she walked across the peninsula to the boathouse. If he sold the peninsula, where would they live? But if he wouldn't see anybody, he'd never be able to sell it. But if he got better—

At that thought, Clothilde shriveled up inside herself at the ugliness in her own heart. She couldn't even learn her lesson, she thought, shriveled up like a worm inside herself. If she really were God, the world would be in a horrible mess. Because now she only wanted to have this third thing over with, however bad it was going to be, so it would all be over and done with. There didn't even have to be a third thing, even if she did have to lose her peninsula. And now she thought of it, she'd be willing to do that—to trade off the Point so the Voice would stop its joke on her. She would, she really would be willing to give it up; that would be fair, she thought desperately.

She sent her thoughts upward. *I will,* she thought. *I promise. I will.*

Even under the fall of warm sunlight, the boathouse crouched on its rocky bed, the door closed. Clothilde knocked and was answered by the same waiting, empty silence. She didn't let herself scare herself with her imagination. She didn't give herself time. She pushed at the door, scraping it across the floor, and marched right in. She would put the box on the table and take the dish and get out, fast.

She didn't even look around. She fixed her eyes on the table and took the three steps to it, where it sat in the middle of the dim room, with the covered dish on it. She dropped the box on the tabletop and picked up the bowl.

But the bowl was heavy. She lifted the cloth and could see that nothing had been eaten. The creamed chicken had turned rancid. He hadn't even eaten the food Mother made for him, she thought, angry, and he hadn't even bothered to throw it out. Then what was he eating? She didn't care.

She dropped the cloth back over the bowl—it was stained now, but he didn't care because he didn't do laundry—and turned to leave.

The dark shape on the bedroll didn't move. It didn't have to move. She recognized it. He was there, his back against the wall, staring at her. A face like that couldn't have any expression, she thought, turning her eyes away; but she couldn't see it anyway, she thought, because of all the shadows. Sunlight couldn't get into the room much, with the high dirty windows to keep it out.

For a second, Clothilde stood there with her head bent down so she didn't have to look at him. The man didn't move either; he just hunched there against the wall.

Clothilde felt like walking out, away. But she couldn't. "That package came for you," she said. "Mother says she hopes you have already paid for it." That was an ugly thing to say, and she didn't know why she had to say such an ugly thing.

He didn't answer, but he got up. She saw him, out of the corner of her vision. She was looking at the floor, and at the covered bowl in her hands, the food he hadn't even touched. They would have liked creamed chicken, over rice, for a supper, and now nobody would be able to eat it.

Out of the corner of her eye she saw him standing by the

window, where, if she looked, she'd have to see him. He was trying to make her look at him. He was trying to drive her away, to make her go away. He was trying to scare her.

Clothilde refused to budge. Her shoes were planted on the wooden floor, and the boathouse was planted on the rocks.

"Nate has run away to live with Grandfather," she said. That was his fault too, this man's fault, so he should know about it.

"Then Nate's a fool," the man said. "You can tell your mother, my father will have to give up my money. I went to a lawyer. The lawyer will get it for her."

"But Mother said—" That was why they were going to have to let Lou go.

"I thought I could surprise her. It was a foolish idea, trying to make her happy."

In her anger at him, Clothilde automatically looked at him. Before she could remember and look away, she saw his face. His face was like the cove at low tide, with the water gone entirely out. Usually, water lay over the cove and hid the floor of it, the rough mud-colored floor, scarred with gullies, pitted with clam breathing holes, and the dark splotches where colonies of mussels spread out. When the water lay over the cove, it could be smooth or serene, or moving under wind the way expressions moved over a face. This face had no expression, and never would be able to, as if the tide had gone out and never would come back. His eyes looked dark, dark blue in the shadows. She wanted to look away. She wished she'd never looked. But she couldn't look away and he was looking right back at her.

It was horrible, as if she could see right through his eyes across his brain and down into his heart—and it was all like that drawing on the wall, cold and bare, and the black shadows falling.

"Tell her that," he said. "Tell her she doesn't have to worry. I've set the lawyers on him, like a pack of dogs."

Clothilde just nodded her head. The bowl in her hands was heavy, the dinner Mother had prepared so carefully for him. The dinner he hadn't even touched. And he could have told Mother, too, and then Mother wouldn't have told them false news. She turned to leave. Because if Mother hadn't told them that false news, things never would have happened that had happened. Things she had made happen.

At the door she turned around. She couldn't have said why, except Mother had said he would know about voices and she needed to know.

When she turned, he already had his back to her, and was looking out the window. He was tall enough to look out of it. All she could see was the back of him, his tall broad shape in a soldier's shirt and trousers, the back of his head with his hair grown shaggy. "People heard voices," she said. "They used to. Was there anyone who ever heard just one voice?"

He turned around again, but the light behind him kept his face in shadows. "Why do you want to know?"

Clothilde didn't have to answer that.

"Are you going crazy, stuck here in this Godforsaken place." He didn't say it like a question, so she didn't have to answer it like a question.

"It's not Godforsaken," Clothilde said. She saw in her imagination the mittened hand, with its clawed fingers digging into the ocean—her peninsula. "It's beautiful," she said, thinking of the water crashing up against the fallen rocks, the tall swaying birch trees and their high waving leaves.

"Is it," he said, another nonquestion. Then—as if he were giving up some battle he was too tired to fight anymore—he said, his whole voice tired, "Maybe it is. Maybe. Socrates did, he's the only one I know, outside of the Bible."

"Who's Socrates?"

"In ancient Greece. He heard a voice he called his

daimon. He said it only told him No. When not to do things and when things weren't true. He said it never told him Yes, so he learned to just listen for the negatives, and I guess he hoped, when he didn't hear them, that he was acting and speaking rightly."

"What happened to him?"

"They put him to death."

"Because he was crazy?"

"No. Because he wanted to speak and act rightly," the man said. "Go away," he added.

But Clothilde had more questions.

"Go away," he said again, dangerous now, even though he stayed still as a shadow.

She left, but she didn't close the door behind her. Let him close the door himself. She ran clumsily up the hill from the boathouse, never minding the way the rancid creamed chicken slopped and slipped, spilling over onto her apron and falling to the ground. She'd be laundering it herself. At least, she did her own laundry.

14

CLOTHILDE didn't want to wake up. The wind, blowing into her room—the wind and the bright sunlight forced her eyes open. She tried to close them. She tried to fall back into forgetting sleep. The wind blew, mixing leaf sounds and water sounds. She sat up in bed.

It was Friday. In town—early, so as to be in time for the morning train from Ellsworth—Tom Hatch would have loaded Lou's family's trunk into the wagon and they would have driven away, inland. Friday was the day they were leaving, returning to Fall River. Clothilde didn't know what Lou might be feeling, traveling back to the mills. She couldn't imagine, except that she knew how she would be feeling herself, if she were leaving the peninsula forever behind her. Imagining that, Clothilde got out of bed.

She didn't look at herself in the bathroom mirror. They had buried Mr. Small and Mr. Twohey yesterday. Nobody from the Point had gone to the service, or to the little graveyard; it wouldn't have been proper. But even if it had been proper, Clothilde couldn't have gone, knowing what she knew. She braided her hair tight, so tight it hurt her scalp. It should never have come asking her, that Voice. And the man in the boathouse, she didn't know what was due to happen to him.

She pulled on a sweater over her blouse and laced her shoes up impatiently. She wanted to get out of her room and out of the house, to get away. She wasn't hungry. Her stomach was a flat board of nonhunger; she couldn't even remember what hunger felt like. If Mother tried to make her eat something—and she would—Clothilde might just be sick. There wasn't any way Mother could force her to open her mouth, put a spoon into it, and swallow. She better not try, Clothilde thought, clattering down the steep stairs.

She had slept late. It was after nine o'clock. Mother was at the kitchen sink, washing her hands. Dierdre sat unhappily at the table, her face newly scrubbed, her hair in French braids, tears hanging from her eyelashes. Clothilde didn't sit down.

"You're too late. I was going to make a chowder, but there won't be another low tide until late evening," Mother said, her voice muffled by running water, and because she was speaking with her back to Clothilde.

All Clothilde could have said about that was I'm sorry, so she didn't say anything. "What's wrong?" she asked Dierdre.

"I don't know what we'll eat for supper," Dierdre said. At the thought, her eyes filled with tears again, and the tears spilled over. "Mother won't tell me."

Why wouldn't Mother tell her? And why did Dierdre have to cry about something that hadn't even happened yet? "We've got bacon, there's fried bread and bacon. You like that," she reminded her little sister.

Dierdre's fresh dress and little white pinafore, and hair subdued into stiff braids, and her scrubbed face—all looked as if she were going to go to a tea party. But Dierdre wasn't going to a tea party. What was she supposed to do with her day, dressed like that? Her eyes looked big and sad. "I wanted chowder," she said. "Mother said. With crispy things."

Dierdre got down from her chair and stood beside

Clothilde, glaring at Mother. Her little head came no further than Clothilde's hip. Clothilde didn't know what Dierdre expected her to be able to do—you couldn't dig clams except at low tide. It just wasn't possible. But she did know what Dierdre wanted, what Dierdre always wanted. When Dierdre turned around and buried her face in Clothilde's skirt, reaching her arms around Clothilde's legs, Clothilde let her two hands stroke Dierdre's back. Mother stayed at the sink, washing away.

When Mother turned around it was only to hold her hands out to Clothilde. The skin was red with scrubbing, the nails were broken short with garden work. "Just look at them," Mother said, as if she were asking Clothilde to look at a crooked seam or some other bad piece of work.

Clothilde looked at the hands. They looked strong, capable, clever.

"And look at me," Mother said.

Clothilde did. Mother's cheeks were pink from being outside in the wind, and her face was getting brown. Her blue eyes with their dark lashes—Mother looked lost, lost and afraid.

Behind her eyes, Mother looked as if she were lost in some strange country, where nobody could understand what she was saying, and she couldn't understand where she was supposed to try to go. She looked as if she were a little child who didn't know what to do and was holding her hand out—but there was nobody there to take her hand.

"I look like some working woman," Mother said.

What did Mother expect to look like? After all, she did work. Clothilde felt as if everything were her fault, but it wasn't.

"He didn't marry you because you were a lady," she said to her mother. "He married you because you weren't. If he'd wanted to marry someone like—like the aunts—there were plenty of them in Manfield."

Mother put her hands down and gathered herself up

straight. She was going to reprimand Clothilde, the way a lady should. Dierdre went to take Mother's hand, and stand glaring at Clothilde.

Clothilde didn't let her mother speak. "There's going to be money, he told me yesterday. He hired lawyers, because Grandfather has to pay the trust money. He didn't want to do that, but he did it for you. You don't know what he wants," Clothilde told her mother, right to her face.

She didn't wait to hear anything Mother had to say. She ran out of the kitchen and across the long grass down to the beach. She didn't know why she'd said that to her mother, and she didn't know why she'd talked that way to her mother, and she didn't want to think about it. And she meant what she said, she meant every word.

The tide was up. Waves blew sideways across the cove. The water was dark blue, and the grainy sand sparkled. The rocks she approached, running along the curve of the beach, running into the wind, shone gray and brown. Clouds— great masses of high clouds—blew across the deep blue sky. Clothilde slowed to a walk, looking around her. The bright wind blew over everything. It was a wind from the east, from the broad ocean and the lands beyond, from Europe, where the war had been. When one of the clouds covered the sun, the wind blew its shadow across the beach and out over the water.

Anger blew through her like a shadow. Mother could have told them, but she never had. Mother must have known for months what had happened to the man's face, but she hadn't told Clothilde. She'd never said, either, that Grandfather didn't want them at his house, or that the aunts didn't like them. Clothilde had had to learn that for herself. Clothilde remembered how she had gradually figured it out, not wanting to be hearing and seeing all the little clues, trying not to know. Money, too, Mother hadn't told them about the money troubles. It was as if Mother put things off until the last minute, hoping something would happen. Mother just didn't *do* anything.

Clothilde stopped dead in her tracks beside the rocks. Her thoughts rose like rocks before her. *She* did things—and now look at the mess she had made. Besides, if you thought about it, all the things she'd done were selfish, all the things she asked for. No wonder she had caused so much trouble. She knew she had caused it, even if nobody else did. She had no business being angry at Mother when her own heart was so bad.

Her own heart was like a monster, horrible to look at, selfish and greedy, grabbing onto what she wanted. If her own heart had ever looked in a mirror—Clothilde hadn't even known what a bad heart she had.

She turned around, looking back to the distant farmhouse. As she did that, she saw a sail at the mouth of the cove. A small sailboat was approaching, with a skiff in tow. The sailboat had a bright white mainsail hoisted, and a little white jib. It moved quickly, running on a broad reach. Its hull was painted bright green. The skiff bounced away behind it. The skiff had once been painted white but the paint hadn't been kept up, so it was a dull faded color. They were returning Nate's boat.

Clothilde climbed up behind the rocks to watch. She didn't know if she was hiding or spying. She only knew that looking out from behind the rocks, where she wouldn't be seen, was what she wanted to do.

The two figures on the sailboat must be Bobby and Alex. Both of them wore white again, and she wondered if they ever wore any other color, and how many times a day they changed into clean clothing, and how many servants they kept busy doing their washing, so that they could always appear in fresh white shirts and trousers. One figure was at the tiller, one handled the main sheet. They sailed into the cove and then dropped sail, with the sailboat's nose pointed up into the wind. They hauled the skiff up and then tied it to the mooring.

With the skiff moored, they didn't sail out again. Instead, they kept the sailboat tied to the skiff, so it wouldn't drift, and sat down low in the cockpit, as if they were hiding. The sails ruffled with the wind. Clothilde saw one of the boys take a thin tube, and put it to his eye—a spyglass. Half-hidden in the boat, the boys took turns lifting their heads to inspect the farmhouse. Once, one of them jumped up and waved his arms wildly, as if he were daring somebody on shore to notice him. He fell abruptly back down.

Clothilde looked at the farmhouse, but she couldn't see anything moving. With a spyglass, though, you could see greater distances, maybe even peep into an open door.

If she had a gun, Clothilde thought, she would shoot it at the boat, if she knew how to shoot it. What kind of friends did Nate have, anyway. Suspicious friends, who didn't entirely believe what he told them. They were right, too, because what he'd told them wasn't the truth.

The world was filled with bad-hearted people, Clothilde thought. No wonder Mother felt lost.

After a while, the boys grew tired of their game, untied the sailboat, hoisted the sails, and went out of the cove. Clothilde, standing up from her crouching position, hoped they would capsize on their way back, or run onto one of the rocks that rose up from the floor of the bay. That rock would rip into the bright green hull, and bite through the wood. They'd be thrown into the water, and the boat sunk, and serve them right. If she were God, Clothilde thought—

She turned and scrambled up the rocks, as if she were running away from something. It felt as if she were running away. When she climbed up over the last rock, her hands scraped by how hard she had clutched at the stones in her ascent, she didn't even look back.

She would walk all over the peninsula, every inch of it.

The fields of timothy and alfalfa—the woods—the quiet glades in the middle of pines and spruces and birch, where pools of sunlight fell—the rocky headlands, one after the other—and the rough open spaces where blueberries were coming to ripeness—always before, when she walked around her peninsula, a kind of peace had come up into her heart. It was as if every time she put her foot down, the quiet flowed up from the ground.

The high blueberry fields first, Clothilde decided, setting off, waiting—inside herself—for the peacefulness to begin. She could hear nothing but the wind, blowing.

Mine, she said out loud to herself, even though she knew it wasn't true, as she stepped into the windy woods. The leaves whispered, rustled. Sometimes, with a sound like a human voice, the branches creaked, groaned.

Clothilde was hungry, and she'd brought no food. She would just have to be hungry. She almost smiled with the satisfaction of wanting food and saying No to herself.

15

At last, Clothilde sat on the rough ground of the headland, her face into the wind. She watched the shadow of a cloud come across the surface of the water. It enveloped the islands and then moved on, driving the brightness ahead of it. It wrapped itself around her.

She had walked the whole peninsula, from its narrow wrist out to this fingertip, skipping only that part where the burned cottage stood. She had paced the edges of the fields of timothy and alfalfa and stood on the rocks that cropped up among the ground-hugging blueberry plants. She had made her way through tangled woods, putting her hand, sometimes, against the peeling bark of a birch. It was no good. None of it did any good. The feeling was no longer there. If she hadn't been so shadowed by sorrow, she would have been sad.

The cloud's shadow blew away, leaving bright windy air filled with the careless water sounds and bird cries, and the rush of wind in her ears, but Clothilde sat wrapped in her own thoughts. She almost wanted the Voice to come back, so she could tell it or ask it or plead with it to please stop. But she never wanted to hear that Voice again. It was dangerous, that Voice.

The land, her peninsula, had nothing to give her any longer. Because it wasn't hers, she thought. If it wasn't hers now, then it never had been hers, even if a will gave it to her. Great-Aunt Clothilde had paid money for it, so she owned it, and could leave it to Clothilde in her will—but Clothilde knew now that the peninsula had nothing to do with money, or with wills, or the laws behind them either.

But if laws and wills and money couldn't make things yours, what could? If you couldn't own things, what could you be sure of? With the peninsula gone from under her feet, Clothilde felt as if she were floating, drifting, through a black night; and falling too, with a terrible speed, and there wasn't anything she could hold on to. If she reached out her hand, her fingers would only grasp emptiness.

She couldn't go on sitting there, sitting still. If she was going to feel this way, she thought she might as well go back to the farmhouse and do something, something useful. Mr. Henderson delivered milk on Fridays, and eggs, and butter; she could go back and set the milk into jars, then wait until the cream had risen, and then pour that off into the smaller cream jar. She could, she thought—standing up and pulling her skirt down straight, brushing wrinkles out of it—finish taking apart the cloak, although how she would get the fabric to Lou now, she didn't know. But if she finished that chore this afternoon, what would she do for the long evening?

She moved quietly back through the woods, still hoping even though she knew there was no use to hope. She took an unaccustomed route, not her own path. She couldn't get lost; she knew the peninsula too well for that; if she didn't know precisely where she was, with the woods closing in around her, she always knew her direction.

When she came to a small open glade in the woods and saw papers scattered around the ground, with a big wooden box of paints open, she almost turned away. Only curiosity led her to step into the sunlit glade, once she had made sure no one was there, and no one nearby. She recognized the size of that wooden box and saw colors on the scattered papers. She was too curious to just walk away.

In the woods, the wind was quieter, having spent some of its energy pushing its way through the trees. The papers on the ground occasionally rustled along, like leaves in the fall. Clothilde stood above them, looking at what they might be.

He was painting the ground, mostly, as if he were lying flat on his stomach to look at the ground. Sometimes, he had done three or four pictures of exactly the same thing, and she could see—by how much was included and the changes between pictures—which he had done last.

Clothilde had never looked so closely at the ground as he was doing when he painted it. In one picture, three birch trees had grown up close together, but two of them had been blown down. She could see which of the logs on the ground had come from which broken trunk. In another, clusters of red berries rested on their clustered green leaves above the tangle of twigs and pine needles and sharp gray stones that covered the ground. Looking at that one, Clothilde caught at her breath, and hunkered down beside it. One cluster, just one, and its four leaves too, casting shadows on one another—if she were ever to see that same cluster she would recognize it. He had made it so absolutely itself when he painted it, that for a minute Clothilde was taken back to the afternoon on the headlands, after the Voice had left her and she could see.

She made herself look at the other pictures, wondering if he had done that almost magical thing at any other time. In a picture of the whole glade, one of the many tree trunks—an old pine, lichen-covered, spiny bare lower branches sticking out—was entirely itself, and the lichen colony too was itself. So he could do it—whatever it was—more than once. He had done it only twice that she could find, crawling among the sheets of paper, entirely absorbed; but he had done it more than once.

She pulled those two thick pieces of paper toward her, and sat cross-legged, looking at them. The bright red groundberries—if she could learn to feel with her eyes as she did with her fingers, she would be able to feel their hardness and roundness and smallness, each one complete. That tree trunk—she could see the years of growing, as if she could see inside it and count its rings, she could feel its reaching upward and how it spread out its high branches.

She hadn't heard footsteps, not so that they registered in her brain and gave her time to run away, but the shadow falling over the two papers didn't surprise her.

"What are you doing here?" his voice demanded.

It's mine, Clothilde almost answered. She didn't look at him. "I'm sorry," she said. Then, although she didn't plan to say anything more, the words came out of her mouth as she stood up and turned around, her eyes on the ground. He'd come sneaking up on her and now he was making her feel as if she had no business being on her own peninsula. "Where were you, anyway?"

His voice laughed but she didn't look to see what his mouth was doing. "I went to relieve myself, if you must know. If you're so curious."

"Oh," she said. Her cheeks grew hot. "Oh." She should have known better than to ask, she thought, and it served her right.

"Is there anything else?" He was still standing there right in front of her, as if he were daring her to look right at him.

"No." Clothilde shook her head. His heavy shoes were covered with mud, the leather scraped in many places, the toes scuffed bare of color. "I don't think so. It wasn't—"

He had waited there as long as he could. He moved away. He stood farther away from her, still facing her, but not looming close.

"Clothilde," he said. "I wouldn't take the Point away from you, I won't if I can help it. Aunt Clothilde wanted you to have it—for some reason of her own she never bothered to explain."

At that she did look at him, and quickly away. His skin looked rough, hard, painful; it looked like muddy sharp rocks, not skin.

"I don't remember her at all," she said.

"I do; she was easy to remember—loud, bossy, bold. And quarrelsome. I enjoyed her visit."

"She must have liked you," Clothilde said.

"Me? No, she didn't. She didn't think much of men, and I was the kind of man she thought least of. My father—she didn't like him either but he could stand up to her. She wasn't interested in me at all."

She looked at him again, briefly, and the mouth was smiling, as she had guessed.

"I don't know what she saw in you," he said, "except being a namesake, but—whatever it was, she saw it. The Point is yours. You have my word—"

Clothilde felt his words being true, as if he could give it back to her, and had done that. She could feel the land beneath her feet rising up from the center of the earth, for her to stand on. She knew that it had been there, that way, all morning too, if she had been able to feel it. If she had been able to feel the way he had been able to see twice in his pictures, she would have felt it.

The man from the boathouse waited, as if she should say something, but she didn't know what to say, standing there. So she asked him, pointing, "Those berries."

"Yes, I saw you studying my little efforts," he said, bitterness in his voice.

"No, those—" She picked up the paper and took it over to him, pointing out to him the one particular cluster.

He didn't say anything, tall beside her. She'd forgotten how big he was. He looked at where her finger pointed until she let her finger drop.

"Was there anything else?" he asked. She knew what he

wanted to say; she knew he wasn't asking her if there was anything else she wanted, in the way you said that to people to tell them it was time for them to go. She knew it, just as he knew—however queerly she'd said it—what she was telling him about the berries. She could feel him forgetting, for a minute, about his monster face. He forgot, for just that minute, so entirely that he didn't even remember he was forgetting something.

"Yes," she answered. She put the paper she held into his hand and picked up the second one. "This." Her finger touched the tree trunk; and her finger could almost feel the scratchiness of the lichen.

"Well," he said, standing beside her. "Well, well. You've got an eye, haven't you."

She shook her head. "It's you. You did it twice," she explained, asking.

"I know what you mean," he said, his voice like water, deep and glad and full of wonder. He did know.

A gust of wind blew through the woods, pulling at Clothilde's skirt and the papers they held in their hands. It blew away the communication between them, too. Without looking, Clothilde felt him remember again. He remembered his face and moved away from her. He gathered up the blowing papers. He put a rock on them, to hold them, and then walked away from her. Across the way he sat down, leaning his back against a tree, with the pad of paper on his knees. He didn't look at her. He sat so that if she stayed she'd have to look at him. He was waiting for her to go away. Clothilde just stood there.

"Was there anything else?" he asked, cold and distant, and meaning to be rude.

Clothilde sat down, leaning against her own tree. She sat and stared at him. He was only pretending to be drawing, she knew that. He was only pretending he didn't notice that she was there. Over his head, the wind pulled along the leaves and the leaves moved helplessly; it looked as if the wind were trailing sunlight, like fire, along the leaves, and they were twisting and pulling to get away from the way the fire hurt them.

"It's not your face," she said. She didn't know why she was saying that because—as he lifted his face in surprise to look at her—she saw how the thick unfeeling skin had grown over it. "You're just—she doesn't care about your face."

He knew what she meant, he knew who she meant. He was angry too, because he didn't want her to talk about it.

Clothilde leaned forward and told him, right to his face, letting him go ahead and be angry: "It's not. And you know it."

His blue eyes glared at her, and she glared right back.

"I saw that picture," she said, proving her point.

"The self-portrait?" he asked. "While you were snooping around?" That wasn't the picture Clothilde had meant but he rushed on, not giving her a chance to correct him. "I suppose you'd call this a handsome face then, a face a woman and a little girl could love?"

"It's a horrible face," Clothilde yelled at him. "And you know it."

As soon as she'd said it, she was sorry. She should never have said that to him. He couldn't do anything about his face and she'd yelled at him, as if it were his fault. But she couldn't stop herself. "It was the other picture I meant. You don't know everything." Clothilde jumped up. Let him just—stay here. She wasn't about to.

He stopped her by laughing. His laughter she had remembered; she didn't know until she heard it how well she had remembered it. Hearing it stopped her feet and turned her around again. But she wasn't going to apologize.

"Where are you running away to?" his laughing voice asked. Then the laughter flowed away, and he said, "Sit down. If you want to. You don't have to go, unless you have to go?"

Clothilde sat down again.

"It was a terrible thing," he said. "War. The war. Just being. . . ." He was looking at her now, and she was looking at him.

"I know," she said, remembering that black wave she had briefly drowned in.

He shook his head. She couldn't know, he knew that. He was right, too; and she knew that too.

"Your grandfather was right—I never should have taken Bucephalus. You know, I'm the one who shot him. I had to. It was—" Clothilde's head nodded because she had understood the sketch he'd sent to them. "He trusted me, and he never should have. It never frightened him, not even at the worst of it. He should never have come with me. I should never have taken him. I was the terrible thing," he said.

Clothilde knew how he felt. The worst things weren't outside of you; no matter how bad they were. "I know," she whispered.

"I earned this face," he said. "It's my face."

Clothilde shook her head.

"I didn't want to come here," he said, gently now, "but I have responsibilities. It would have been easier not to—bring myself here. Some things you do, you can't ever undo them, or make up for them," he said, gently still.

"But it wasn't what you wanted to do," she protested, reminding him. "You didn't mean for Bucephalus to die."

He didn't answer. He knew she didn't need to be answered. He started sketching again, and for a few minutes forgot she was there. Clothilde sat watching him, feeling how well he'd forgotten that she was there with him. It wasn't that he'd turned his back on her, it was that he was sketching.

Shadows ran over them, and sunlight, while she watched. When he finally looked up it was to apologize. "I'm sorry," he said, meaning, she thought, sorry to have forgotten her.

"I don't mind," she answered. "But you ought to come back. Home. To the house, to live with us. Nate's gone."

"You told me," he reminded her. "But you have to think of your sister. Dierdre. I'd give her bad dreams."

That was true, probably, Clothilde thought, maybe. "There's a man, he's in a bad way because of the war, as if his mind. . . ." She couldn't explain it. She tried to ask him another way. "He said—he sounds crazy but—I guess he is, but—"

The man waited, watching her. Then he said, "After the doctors were through with me, they sent me to another hospital. It was in England. I was there a year, more than a year I think, I can't remember. After a while, I talked to a lot of men there, who talked crazy."

"Jeb told me, things that grow down love the rain; and things that grow up love the sunlight." She wanted the man to tell her which he was, so she could know it. She didn't mind which he was, as long as she could be sure of it.

The man watched her, and considered. "He sounds like a gardener to me. Is he a farmer?"

That wasn't what Clothilde had wanted to know, not at all. She shrugged. "He doesn't do anything, he can't. He's really in a bad way, he can't do anything. He gets frightened, and—"

"I think," the man said, setting his sketchbook down, "that I'm both. Or maybe I'm shadows, which is part of the above-ground world."

"When he said it—he thinks he's below ground."

"I can understand that," the man said.

"So can I," Clothilde agreed.

He laughed again, and asked her, teasing now, "And when did you get so wise?"

She didn't answer that. And she didn't think she was wise, anyway. Neither did he, teasing her, and she smiled at the teasing; but he didn't know. "Nate *shouldn't* have gone," she said. Nate had just run away, and not tried; he hadn't even given the man any time.

"You can't blame him. After all, your grandfather has a lot to offer."

"He doesn't have anything," Clothilde said. "And you know that as well as I do, Father."

"Clothilde!" He sounded shocked, but his mouth was smiling and his eyes, too, were smiling, in the old way, in his new face. "How can you say that about the man who has the most magnificent mausoleum in Mansfield, Massachusetts?"

Clothilde couldn't stop herself—it just made her laugh, what he said, and the way he said it. She'd been taken to the cemetery to see that mausoleum, which looked like a tiny palace with pillars and scrolls and the name, SPEER, carved over the doorway. It was all out of proportion, that building—huge and ugly for a grave, but ridiculously small and heavy for a palace. Laughing, she got to her feet. "You ought to come home," she told her father.

He shook his head.

"At least, in the evenings," she insisted. "For Mother."

He couldn't answer her. Words were tangling up in his throat, she could feel that. She made herself, now that she was up, take the long five short steps across to him. She made herself bend over and kiss his face. She didn't want to do that and he sat stiff and still, as if he was helpless to stop her.

When she'd kissed the face once, she felt so sorry for him she kissed him again, because she loved him and wanted him to be happier than he could be. She felt his strong arms go around her. Just for a minute, selfishly, she let herself feel her father's strong arms around her.

She looked right at him, from close, when she pulled away. He looked right back at her, and she didn't know what he was thinking.

"I could have lost my eyes," her father said. "That was a possibility. And I didn't."

"You really ought to be home," she said.

This time he answered. "Maybe."

Clothilde went back through the woods, cutting across to her own path. He would be drawing again already, she was willing to bet. Maybe, if he drew a picture of a little girl, like Dierdre, with a man who was himself, and the picture showed how the man loved the little girl—like Beauty and the Beast. If he gave that picture to Dierdre—he could draw it, she was sure of that.

She almost turned around to go back to him with that idea. She didn't though, because he'd be sitting and sketching. She remembered it like a picture, a painting of the glade surrounded by trees, the sky overhead and the bright air blowing around the scene, with the quiet man sitting there. He sat there so concentrated on drawing what he saw that he didn't see what he saw.

Clothilde knew that he shouldn't be disturbed. And she suddenly knew—knew so deeply and entirely that she broke out crying, tears bursting out of her eyes as sudden as rain—that he was getting better, that he was going to get better. Not his face, but the important thing. His face would always stay the same, she knew that. But the important thing—inside him—was healing.

Her legs collapsed underneath her, but the ground caught her and held her safe until she had cried herself out.

16

T HE next morning, Clothilde awoke before first light. She had been very deeply asleep, with the blankets wrapped around her like a pair of arms. Then she was wide awake, and out of bed. She dressed hastily but carried her shoes in her hand. In the dark kitchen, she put on the shoes and cut herself a big piece of the coffeecake she had made yesterday. She had baked the sweet cake for Father, kneading it, layering the dough with slices of apples sprinkled with sugar and cinnamon and nutmeg, to serve to Father, should he come to call.

He hadn't come, not last night. He might not come again tonight, she knew. She wasn't worried about her cake: if it wasn't eaten tonight, it would be eaten for breakfast tomorrow, before they set off to Sunday morning services. If it was eaten tomorrow for breakfast, she would bake another in the afternoon, for Father, should he come to call.

Father would, one day, come home; she knew that. She didn't doubt him. Clothilde, stepping outside into the morning, bit into the chunk of cake. It tasted good, so good that she hoped Father would choose tonight to make the attempt. She would like to give him a slice of this cake that she had made, because it was sweet and fresh and good, because she had made it.

The tide was out, the water distant, calm. Predawn light silvered the mud flats. The tumbled rocks lay like a pirate's treasure of tarnished silver bowls, with the seaweed draped over them like stolen necklaces. Clothilde climbed up and over the rocks, to enter the woods. She followed her own path through the lightening air.

At the headlands, as the sun rose, she stood. There was no wind and the air was cool, with warmth behind its coolness. Off to the east, in pale whites and pinks and yellows, the sun rose. The sun painted the water beneath; the sun spread out colors before itself. Sunlight brought color to the islands, to trees, rocks and lighthouse. The water reflected the brightening blue of the sky with its own deeper shades. Clothilde stood, and waited.

As the morning went on, she sat and waited. Birds awoke, and the tide came silently in, rising. Cormorants, gulls, three swimming seals, and the white sails of one of the yachts from over town moved across the water, as she waited. She waited impatiently, and then through her impatience. She waited stubbornly, as the air warmed and the morning moved on, the sun rising along the arc of the sky. The air was warm at midmorning, but there was a coolness behind it as she sat waiting through her own stubbornness.

The waves moved below her. She watched them—each one separate and distinct, each one making its own flowing design. Each wave she watched she lost track of, in the whole dancing movement of the water. The slow-moving tide rose up on the rocks, and the slow-moving sun rose up the sky to its noonday height. Clothilde felt as if it were always one moment she was occupying, the waiting moment. The slow-moving morning went by, minute by minute, and Clothilde sat silent in the same moment of waiting.

With the sun so high overhead that there were no shadows, she knew she was no longer waiting. The wave her eyes followed in its dancing journey to shore had sudden deep colors of blue and green and brown; as she watched, she saw it join in with its fellows, saw it both separate and part, saw it both at the same time.

There was no need to hear her name called. She stood up, her hands clasped together behind her. "Thank you," she said. "Thank you for my father."

"Who?" the Voice wondered.

Remembering, Clothilde named him: "Benjamin Speer."

"Yes," the Voice said, in her ear, all around her. "And the others?"

Clothilde didn't answer that. If she had, her answers would have been only questions, Whys, and What's-going-to-happens.

The Voice waited, and then asked her, "Are you answered?"

"Yes," she said. She didn't like the answer, but she knew now she couldn't understand; that knowledge was her answer. She wanted to protest, but didn't dare.

"Ask," the Voice asked.

"Lou—Louisa Small." Clothilde didn't know how she dared to think of asking for something else, and she was frightened to see—coming into her own mind—even more requests, as if she hadn't understood after all. She wanted something for Lou most of all; but blowing into her mind like a leaf under the wind was the notion of Polly Dethier. Prettier than Polly, that was the wish.

It was Lou to whom she owed what she could do, if the Voice didn't lose patience. But it was so dangerous to ask, and she didn't want to make things worse for Lou. To ask for things, a husband, wealth, happiness—Clothilde could see the dangers in such wishes, however well-intentioned they were. Those were what she wished she could ask for. If she could frame out her whole desire it would be that Lou should marry Tom Hatch, return to the village or maybe even to the peninsula, and have children of her own, living with that good man. Even though it was a good wish, Clothilde knew it was dangerous. Each life, like each wave, or like each leaf—she knew she couldn't understand.

Not wealth then, not happiness. "Strength?" Clothilde asked.

"Strength, yes," the Voice answered.

"Thank you," Clothilde said again. To ask for more would be greedy. There was always more to ask for, to want. She pushed her lips firmly shut and pushed back at the picture of Polly.

Waiting, the Voice waiting, Clothilde wondered if there were something she was supposed to do. She wondered if she should bow her head, or curtsey, if there were some gesture by which she could show that she was finished. Then she remembered and, "I'm sorry," she said. "I'm sorry about Mr. Small, and Mr. Twohey especially, and Nate too. I'm sorry I didn't do better. I should have. Maybe you shouldn't have come to a girl." She didn't want the Voice to think she was giving advice, but she thought maybe the Voice ought to know this.

"Girl?" the Voice sounded surprised.

Maybe it didn't know girl. Or maybe it hadn't noticed. "It doesn't matter," she said, with the unexpectedness of the situation pulling at her mouth, to make it smile, with her smile making her voice as warm as the air around her.

"You do know that I didn't mean—" she started to say, but she stopped herself. She was evading the question. "Am I responsible?" she asked, wanting to be told No.

"Yes. You asked."

She couldn't do anything about that, except learn. If she asked to be prettier than Polly, for example, and Polly—and something happened to Polly. Clothilde blew away at the picture of Polly Dethier with all her strength, and shook her head clear. "I am responsible, aren't I?"

"No," the Voice said. "Amos Small," it spoke the names, "Joseph Twohey, Nathaniel Speer—they chose. So there is no more?" The Voice didn't want her to ask for more. It wasn't trying to trick her into greediness. It was only asking. Clothilde, her lips firmly closed, shook her head. But the Voice was wondering—she could feel that.

"I understand that it's not mine," she said, "Speer Point. The peninsula. This." She felt it firm under her feet, rock upon rock, as she said it.

"Yes," the Voice agreed. "Then there is no more."

Only gratitude, Clothilde thought, looking for the right words to say it.

The Voice had gone before she could find them, and she was alone again. She turned quickly, before she could lose a second of it, to see the woods behind her, every leaf of every branch, every little ground-clinging vine, and the spreading mosses. Even as she watched, they faded back to ordinariness. She didn't grieve, because she had been able—for however many minutes it had been—to see. She didn't grieve, because she knew where she could find the seeing again, not complete but still there: in Father's drawings. The seeing wasn't lost; it was just going to be rare; it would take some seeking.

Clothilde stepped into the woods, to go home. But she hadn't said good-bye. The Voice hadn't said good-bye either. For that matter, she thought, following the sound of her own laughter through the woods, it hadn't said hello. The Voice didn't notice good-bye or hello, she was willing to bet on that.

EPILOGUE

T HAT'S it. That's my story.

It happened a long time ago, as the simplest mathematics will tell you. That's what happened and I've written it down for you to read. The only other person I've ever told it to was my husband. You'll want to know what he thought, because I know how crazy my story sounds. When I finished telling him about that peculiar week in my life, he believed me but he didn't believe it, if you see what I mean. On the other hand, what he said to me about it did surprise me. "You didn't ask why, Clothilde," he said. "What a strange little girl you must have been. Didn't you ever wonder why this happened to you? To you specially?" Well no, I hadn't, and I never thought that made me particularly strange, and I still don't. "Anyway, now I know why you wouldn't agree to marry me until we'd been to Speer Point," he said. "But what would you have done if I'd hated it?" He was no fool, your great-grandfather. I told him it was no good thinking of what might have happened, since it's hard enough making sense out of what did happen. And that was that.

I've written it down for you because I'm getting old now, old enough to know that at any time I may die. Sometimes that knowledge is comfortable to me, as comfortable as this untidy old desk by a window that overlooks the rose gardens that encircle this house. (When the leaves are down in winter, I can just see the roof of the boathouse.) Sometimes that knowledge gives me the jumps. Death frightens me. Well, it's a big change, and if you've read my story you must know that changes have always unnerved me. I will, of course, be dead at the time when this is put into your hands.

I don't know what you'll think. But if I know my family, there will be a lot of questions asked. They'll wonder why I've left Speer Point to you, you of all people. You aren't even a proper Speer. How could you be, when you were already born at the time your mother married my grandson. The Speers have a strong greedy streak, and they'll wonder. If your Great-Uncle Nate survives me—and has all his marbles—he'll speak out for you. He'll be wrong about it, but they'll listen to his explanations of inheritance taxes, and he'll believe it himself. That'll be reason enough for them. I want you to know the real reason.

But if I know children, what you'll really want to know is: Then what happened?

You know what happened to me. Father and I are the two distinguished Speers, the famous ones. The family is proud of us, so you'll have heard more than you want to about us; and the family resents us, too, in the complicated way of families. You already know about me, so I can only add what they don't know, or don't know the significance of.

The peninsula—obviously, it remained in my hands, because otherwise I couldn't now put it into yours. It was money from selling timber that paid my college bills. We harvested the older, larger trees, pines and spruces, maples; then we replanted. Some of the trees that were young when I was a girl will be there for you, should you need them. After college I continued studying; I studied medicine and psychology. I became, as you know, a psychotherapist—

and a fine one, if I'm the one to say so. I turned out to have a talent for seeing inside of people, and I used it. I married, and continued my work, and had children, and continued my work. At first I was criticized for that, and then I was admired, as times changed and opinions changed. My life was intensely interesting to me, but I don't imagine it would be to you.

Father and Mother lived their lives out on Speer Point. When his illustrations began to earn money, they rebuilt the cottage, where I now live alone. Father has become famous as a watercolorist, but his illustrated books earned his living. *Beauty and the Beast* was his first success, the old fairy tale. They'll give you that book, when you're old enough. The Speers take to pride easily, and they are proud of Father because his pictures hang in museums. I think it would have amused him, to have been brought back into the center of the family like that; although he did no laughing when Speer Electric Motors went under, half a century ago. Mother finally had her gardens at this house, the flower gardens, but she kept up the kitchen gardens too. Father came home, to live with us, and as the years went by Mother learned to believe that he was glad he'd married her, which gave her all the contentment she wanted, between her children, her husband, and her garden.

Jeb Twohey was her gardener. At first, it was only the orchard and vegetable gardens at the farmhouse, and we could pay him only in work, only by giving him work to do. Jeb had hands that made things grow. His dahlias—their colors just exploded into the air. His mind never mended but he worked in peace out at Speer Point.

Nate—as you know, because it's family legend—pulled himself up after the Great Crash by his bootstraps. I'm sure you've heard more than enough about his various struggles. I always thought struggle was the best thing for him, but I don't see that his bitterness has been sweetened any by his later successes. Dierdre grew up and married one of

Father's artist friends, who never gave her much but love—which was all she needed. He went off to the Second War, but came through it safely; Dierdre was kept safe. She raised the basset hounds every Speer who keeps a pet has in his house, and those dogs loved her enough to fill in all her hungry cracks.

Tom Hatch lived and died a bachelor, and a good friend. Polly Dethier—she had her coming-out party, and I went to it. Nate did not accept his invitation. I was miserable, of course, but Polly danced with the young men, and her eyes had that shining hope in them. When she did marry, however, it wasn't to one of the summer boys from town, nor to one of the young men from Bangor. She married the youngest Henderson boy. I went to her wedding and saw how her eyes shone with hope, as she turned around from the minister to look at us. Polly had children and she worked, the way a farmer's wife has to. She and her husband moved into the farmhouse when this house was built; it's their grandchildren who manage the farm and the timber plantations now. Polly never lost her ability to hope. I don't know if that was a blessing to her or not—how much she could hope, no matter how many old hopes were dashed—but I got to admiring that quality in her.

I tried to find Lou, tried to have her come back, but I never did. I wrote letters, but there was never any answer. Lou couldn't read or write, so I don't even know what it meant that there was no answer. Nobody in the village knew her address in Fall River, or the name of her mother's sister. We didn't know which of the mills she worked at, so I wrote to each. There was never any answer. We didn't know which of the many churches there was hers, although our minister wrote to find her. With the money from the first timber cutting, Father hired a detective for me. The detective at least could track her down, and find her name on the employee lists. But she'd gone away five years earlier. She had vanished from the lists, after being employed there for only a year. Where she went to, I've never known and I've always wondered. Sometimes, I've thought it must have been good, her life, because she had strength. Sometimes I've been afraid it must have been bad, to need strength. Every time I think of Lou—like right now—I feel how I need to know, and how I never will.

Finally there's you. If my own experience is anything to go by, you'll want to know why I've left the peninsula to you in my will. Everybody will want to know, but you're the only one who has the right. I'd let the rest of them wonder, if I were you, but then I've always been uncooperative and uncomfortable, to myself and to the people around me. They'll tell you we only met the once, but they won't be able to tell you what it was like for me—the distinguished old lady—to meet the child you were. You refused to come any farther into the room than the doorway, and your mother wanted so badly for you to make a good impression on your new family. She had scrubbed you shiny clean for the wedding, and dressed you up. You hated it, I could see that. You hated the way the family was studying you, and studying your mother. She had shined your shoes as bright as your cheeks, and you had the big eyes little children have, standing there with your feet planted on the rug . . . you looked about as miserable as anyone I've ever seen. I recognized those square planted feet of yours, and the sullen little face, and it made me laugh. I was laughing when I said hello, and bent over to shake your hand—me, the grand lady with my white hair and white gloves. I held out my hand for you to shake and you—you looked at me as if you'd like to kick me in the shins. Your mother made the apologizing, purring noises mothers make, and you looked like you wanted to kick her in the shins when you were through kicking me. So I went away, because your poor mother was already at her wit's end with all those Speers in the room and I wasn't helping, trying to get you to like me. I went to talk to somebody else, I can't remember who. But I remember you.

And if that isn't explanation enough, you'll have to find your own. I've given you my story and the peninsula that isn't mine. The rest is up to you.

CYNTHIA VOIGT is the author of twelve books, including Newbery Medal–Winner DICEY'S SONG and Newbery Honor Book A SOLITARY BLUE. She lives in Annapolis, Maryland, with her husband, son, and daughter and their dog. Both Cynthia and her husband, Walter Voigt, teach at a private school.